I0456675

The

Beautiful

Way

BarbarianSpy

www.BarbarianSpy.com

This book is copyright © Dirk Hessian
Dirk Hessian asserts his right to be known as the author of this work
Published by BarbarianSpy in 2012
Cover design © S Bush 2012
Cover images: all manipulated: Geisha © Marianna Kosmina at
Dreamstime.com, man © Raisa Kanareva at Dreamstime.com
ISBN E-book: 978-1-921879-88-3
ISBN Print: 978-1-922187-83-3
All rights reserved

BarbarianSpy
Jindalee St
Toronto, NSW 2283
Australia

The

Beautiful Way

by

Dirk Hessian

Table of Contents

Preface

The life of a male prostitute—a *jinan*—in the Floating World of the Beautiful Way in ancient China in the waning years of the Chu dynasty, 200 BC, was a sensual but cruel, often foreshortened, bitter-sweet existence. *The Beautiful Way* weaves a complex, romantic, and all too often tragic tale of the interwoven lives of six jinan of one male brothel—the Cut Sleeve Nanleshijia. Laid against their linked stories are those of the managers and servants who guided these beautiful young men through their training, their initiation—in which they became bitten peaches—and beyond to burn as bright stars, and, in too many cases, sputter too early to ash.

On the surface, the life of a male courtesan in China twenty-two centuries ago was a lush, pampered existence, and the services they provided, described in this novel, were exotic and arousing. Most young Chinese men of the era were promised only a hardscrabble life fighting the elements for too scant a harvest and sustenance and dying an early death. To be taken into the nanleshijia marked a young man as having certain charms, beauty, and diminutive stature and guaranteed him comfort and nurturing, leading up to a highly formalized deflowering and folding into the life of those who served the demanding sexual needs of powerful men. For the best jinan, it also led to fame, sponsorship, and an assured protected and refined life. But underneath this veneer of vermillion lacquer and refined beauty lay a world of danger, uncertainty, competition, loneliness, and cruelty that became more than most jinan could bear—and certainly more than they deserved just for being born desirable.

While providing an intricate network of stories of adventure, sexual exploits, and entwining relationships, *The Beautiful Way* strives to capture the essence of the deliciously euphemistic Oriental world of men making love to other men in China's ancient past and covering two kingdoms. The stories of these six jinan and of the men who served, coveted, and mastered them are interwoven tales that go beyond the random act of sexual release between men. They offer more complex and context-richer studies by gathering age-old themes, exotic settings, and all-so-human characters up into the Floating World of the Orient. A world in which men give themselves to other men—some more freely than others—for something in return, whether it is money, position, power, survival, honor, service, devotion—or, not all that rarely, really, in unconditional love.

Maneuvering through unfamiliar foreign names and terms can be daunting in reading a novel from "another world," both in time and place. Thus an annotated listing of the novel's identified characters and a glossary of Chinese and key terms are provided at the end of this book.

Chapter One: School for Nantung's Nanleshijia

The caretaker judged that he had been right to do as he had done. The school *baoan*, Niu—The Ox—whose job it was to protect the *nanleshijia*—male pleasure house—students from the outside world, apparently was more of a threat than a protector. The caretaker—the *zhaoguzhe*—knew he must accept responsibility for hiring such a young and volatile man as protector. As the caretaker of these young students, the zhaoguzhe had to make what had come out of harmony right again. Sending young Deming—Virtue Bright—to the monks of Langshan—Wolf Hill—was the first step in this atonement. But the zhaoguzhe could readily tell from Niu's reaction that it would not be enough.

"Where have you sent Deming?" Niu demanded. He rounded on the zhaoguzhe, towering over him, all muscle and power, but knowing that it would be death to so much as touch the manager of the nanleshijia school—the preparation school of Nantung's male pleasure house. "Deming is not sufficiently prepared yet."

"Deming is sufficiently prepared in being arousing to men, wouldn't you say?" zhaoguzhe countered with a hard, accusing look in his eyes. "Deming is fulfilling his destiny, just as any other of those of the Beautiful Way do. He is where he is safe from predators."

"I protect the students here from predators," Niu declared.

"I am well aware of your duties here," said the zhaoguzhe. "Perhaps more than you are. Perhaps I appreciate more what you are supposed to be doing than you do."

"Where—?"

But the zhaoguzhe simply gave Niu a disdainful look and turned and, *hanfu*—ceremonial robes—rustling against the bamboo walls of the narrow passageway into the heart of the male pleasure house, flowed away like one of the majestic ships that the growing riverside village of Nantung was famous for building.

As famous as the port city on the northern bank of the Yangtze River, near its mouth in the kingdom of Wu, was for shipbuilding, it was even more famous for its beautiful and pliable young men. In this era, Wu was the most powerful of the three Middle Kingdoms in military strength, agricultural production, and trade. Most legendary of its trade goods, though, was its supply of youths for the Beautiful Way—the world of male prostitution.

The Cut Sleeve Nanleshijia was not the only male brothel in Nantung, but it was the most expensive one and the one where the richest and most powerful patrons of the prefecture of Yangzhou, in which it was located, were clients. And it also had the most respected preparation school attached to it. Only the most beautiful and refined young men were admitted there, where, for several years, their talents for entertaining and pleasing were even further refined. The training only went so far, however. Every young man went to his first client a virgin, usually in an auction followed by an elaborate ceremony. And large fortunes were paid for the privilege of being the "first" for one of these young men.

That was why the zhaoguzhe had sent the young Deming where he did. He was dissatisfied with what he had

had to do—he had to take less than Deming could normally have earned for his first taking. But the zhaoguzhe knew that time was extremely short before Niu, a very arousing young man in his own right, but a baoan—a protector—rather than a student, ruined Deming for that first entertainment. The inevitable had become obvious when the zhaoguzhe had seen the looks Deming had been giving the muscular body of Niu as the baoan sluiced off his body at the water spout at the end of his working day. Deming could not be trusted to hold himself in check any more than Niu could.

And in this Deming was more at fault than Niu was. Niu was untrained, a virile animal acting on natural instinct. Deming had been trained to control his emotions. For this transgression, Deming had to be punished.

Niu stood there in the passageway, fists clinching, bitter words on his lips, watching the zhaoguzhe sail away from him. He took one step forward, as to follow the zhaoguzhe, but from behind him, a trembling, restraining hand reached out and touched his arm.

"It is useless to badger the old man, baoan. He will not tell you where Deming went. But I know where Deming went. I can take you there."

Niu turned and looked at the school servant, Shun—Obedient—a former student whose arm had been scalded with boiling water in an accident and who no longer was perfect, and thus had been reduced to the level of servant.

"Show me."

The zhaoguzhe watched them leave from the garden pavilion on the cliff overlooking the Yangtze. He smiled. Even though he knew the servant, Shun, was so smitten with the baoan that he would lead Niu to where Deming had been sent, he also knew that Niu would be too late to do anything about it.

From where he stood, he could see down the willow-bordered pathway and thus was able to see that a vermillion palanquin, carried by six sturdy soldiers of the imperial guard of the House of Wu, was approaching. The caretaker moved swiftly back into the nanleshijia and to the room where the youngest and slimmest of the students in preparation,

Xiaodan—Little Dawn—was being clothed and powdered for his trip to Gusu, the capital of Wu.

The zhaoguzhe regretted that he had not had sufficient time to train Xiaodan—he was the most recently arrived of the students—but he had received instructions to provide the most femininely beautiful of his students, and when he demurred on sending who that would be—Xiaodan—because the young man was not yet trained enough in the life of a *jinan*—a male prostitute—he was informed that the most innocent of the students would be the most welcome, trained or not.

After Xiaodan had departed in the palanquin with the training master of the capital city's premier drama troupe, the zhaoguzhe floated into the large salon, where the other students had gathered. Which, he wondered, would be the next to make his way to the outside world? Some would need to remain. The Cut Sleeve Nanleshijia itself would need the best that he could keep back.

He cast his eye on the exotic beauty, Xiu—Fine Beauty. This was the young man who would be the most arousing and who had become the most learned in the ways of arousing other men. If he was at all able, Xiu would remain to become the principle jinan of the house. And if so, the shy and diminutive Bolin—Gentle Rain—would need to remain as well. The two were almost as brothers and were inseparable. Xiu would do anything, if only he knew Bolin was safe and being treated well. And it would seem that Bolin would do nothing, without crying about it, without the present support of Xiu.

The zhaoguzhe's attention went to Ping—Tranquility—who was entertaining the rest with his song and lute. When the drama master at the capital asked for one of the students, Ping had been the first to come to mind. He was the most talented in the arts other than sensual—Xiu reigned supreme there. But a less accomplished artist was what was sought. The zhaoguzhe assumed Ping would go at a high price and bring considerable honor to the nanleshijia school.

Of the rest, the zhaoguzhe could not speculate what would happen to them. He would assign them as needed and convenient.

He stood there, watching them in repose. Which would be the next to leave the nest, he wondered. Something told him that it would have to be the baoan rather than a student. He had averted disaster with Deming, but Niu had also given looks of desire at Xiu, and Xiu was just too valuable of a commodity to let Niu spoil him. No, he thought, it would have to be Niu who left next. He could not be sold as any student would be, but he was owned by the nanleshijia as any of the students were. It would have to be a special arrangement, and it would have to be lucrative enough to make up for the lower price Deming went for.

The zhaoguzhe strolled slowly back to his own offices, his mind spinning out the answer to this puzzle. He actually rather liked puzzles of this nature.

Chapter Two: Niu on Wolf Hill

"Tell me where we are going, Shun."

The servant, Shun, looked about him to make sure that no one who would report back to the zhaoguzhe—the manager—had followed them from the nanleshijia—the male pleasure house. They were at the first rest lookout point on Langshan mountain—Wolf Hill—that rose at the edge of Nantung and was almost encircled by a snake-like bend of the Yangtze, a wide and muddy river at this point. Shun looked out over the picturesque port village of Nantung. The town was built around a series of lakes and was itself almost encircled within a lesser river, the Haohe, that wound around the town in what was called the "Emerald Necklace" and flowed into the Yangtze just below Langshan mountain. It was raining in a drizzle and Shun could barely make out the village below him in the mist—or the upper reaches of the sacred mountain above him. Through a break in the mist farther down the mountain. Through the finger of clouds drifting below where he stood, though, he could see the nanleshijia compound perched on a cliff below them and overlooking the roiling waters of the Yangtze.

"He was sent to the monks of the Dragon Temple at the summit of the mountain, baoan," Shun said. "I overheard the zhaoguzhe say Deming needed to be punished for betraying his training."

"The monks at the Dragon Temple!" Niu exclaimed. "They will ruin him and then take him into the temple as one of them, never to be seen by any of us again. This cannot be."

With that Niu turned toward the stone steps leading up into the mist of the mountain and began to run.

"Careful, baoan," Shun called after him, afraid that the love and want for the muscular protector of the house that had been in his heart for some time would betray him in the tone of his voice. But Niu did not have ears for the lowly nanleshijia servant.

Nearly as soon as Niu disappeared into the mist, though, Shun heard a pained exclamation and the rustling of the fern fronds that bordered the upward stone pathway.

The strangled voice of the baoan called from out of the cloud. "Heavens be cursed, I . . . have fallen."

Shun, with no regard for his own safety now, ran up the stone steps and helped Niu to rise. It was baoan who was supposed to be the strength of the nanleshijia; that he seemed so helpless reflected to Shun how emotionally charged he was at losing the first taking of Deming that he had cultivated for so long.

"More carefully. We must walk more carefully on the slime-covered wet stones," Shun called into the mists. But Niu was not listening. He set off again, limping a bit this time. Shun reached out for the sleeve of the baoan's scarlet-red silk hanfu, but the protector skittered away from him, farther up the rising stone path, anxious to reach his destination, focused on his own goal.

Mere yards farther up the path, Niu almost slipped and went down on the moist, moss-covered stepping stones again. But the young servant, Shun, was there right behind him, placed a strong hand under the arm of the man he loved above all other men, and gently supported him while Niu, unthinking of his own safety, continued up the steep ascent.

"I have you, baoan," Shun murmured. "I shall not let you fall."

Lost in his burning need, Niu paid Shun no heed.

Of course Shun wouldn't let the baoan fall. That went without saying. In fact, most of what Shun did for Niu went without acknowledgment.

"Where . . . Where are you, Deming?" Niu cried out, looking frantically up the path, wanting to catch at least a last glimpse of the one he loved deeply—but of course wanting so much more. Langshan—Wolf Hill—and the monks of the Dragon Temple would have been snatching Deming from Niu soon enough. Niu could not prevent that. The assignment of Deming could not be altered. But Niu could reach him first and quench this fire in his belly for the flower of Deming before the monks did their worst. Niu had an obsession to be the first with any young man who aroused him.

Once more, despite his sprained ankle, Niu surged ahead of Shun up the pathway. He was strongly built and powerful. No one in Nantung could match his strength—or his determination to make the summit of the mountain. It was a miracle that Shun was able to support him as he had been called to do more than once on this trek up the mountain—but his devotion had given him superhuman strength as well.

As Niu climbed toward the last resting terrace for the public, called the parting stones, where no one not invited to proceed by the priests of the Dragon Temple was permitted to pass, Shun called out to Niu, who surely must have had to stop before reaching there for a rest. But there was no answer. Niu had already gone ahead.

Shun began to shudder, his whole world coming down around him. He looked up the mountain, trying to pick out the accursed temple, but unable to do so through the tops of the pine trees and the swirling blanket of misty clouds sitting upon the summit of Langshan.

"Let them already have initiated Deming and taken him into the temple," Shun prayed—but silently, of course. It would be a tragedy for him for Niu to hear what was in Shun's heart.

Hearing a grunt of pain above, but near, propelled Shun up the mountain. He found Niu slumped on the stones, rubbing his chin. "Here, lean on me, baoan," the servant Shun whispered to him. "We can move faster if I take your weight upon me."

And without a word, Niu let Shun put a steadying arm under his and, using strength he should not have, lift him and thus move at a quicker and more steady pace up the ever-sharpening angle of ascent.

This was not what he wanted, Shun was agonizing as resolute and steady on the slippery stepping stones, he helped Niu up the stairs. Shun wanted Niu for himself. But the baoan only had eyes for the beautiful students in preparation to be jinan—male prostitutes—in the nanleshijia. Niu cared nothing for the young man with the scalded arm, the less than perfect man. Shun would give his arm entirely if Niu would cast an aroused eye on him. Even though that was not happening, Shun would support Niu in anything he wanted to do.

Niu, supported on the imperfect arm of Shun, reached the last rise of the mountain and stopped at the small stone terrace, the parting stones, which was surrounded by stone benches, bordered by lacy-leafed maple trees sighing in the breeze floating up from the base of the Langshan. A stone path led up farther from here, straight up for a few feet and then taking a sharp turn to the right and disappearing behind closely planted pine trees. The mists of the early morning dipped down at this point to make a low ceiling to the small stone terrace. Beyond this point no one was sanctioned to go who was not initiated in—or about to be initiated into—the Dragon Temple.

Niu sank down on the stone bench. Shun crouched nearby, ready to lend any aid to his master that he was asked to provide. Niu sobbed openly, unashamedly, letting all of his grief pour out of him. He had not been able to reach Deming before he was taken up to the summit.

As Niu grew silent, his desperation wrung out of him, he heard it. The sound of lilting music, not just the breeze playing through the leaves of the pines and the lacey-leafed maples, but a haunting tune on some sort of flute. It was coming from farther up the mountainside, beyond the upper, forbidden stone terrace.

Niu struggled to his feet and limped toward the pathway leading up from the stone terrace.

"What is it, baoan?" Shun asked in a low, throaty voice. "I hear music. Is that what you hear? Do you intend to mount the Langshan farther. We are not permitted . . . oh, here, give me your arm. If you wish to climb farther, I was support you. I'll help you wherever you want to go."

Niu gave no indication that he even heard Shun, but he leaned on the young man's arm quickly enough regardless and let the servant support him on the upward, steeper climb into the mists of the morning.

They had almost reached another, larger stone terrace near the summit, nearly fully shrouded in clumps of white, wispy clouds, when they distinctly heard the flute playing—and the low beat of a drum—and also heard the rustling and slapping of many sets of bare feet, scurrying across a parallel pathway around the near summit of the mountain that intersected with the upward path to this larger stone terrace.

Niu and Shun instinctively drew back and crouched down into the dewy patch of ferns within a thickly planted copse of pine, where they could see up to the stone terrace but, with luck, could not be seen. Legend had it that no one who journeyed beyond the parting stones who was not of the temple community or being initiated into it returned to the valley alive. So, intoxicated and driven Niu and loyal-to-the-death Shun had continued their upward journey filled with great fear and trembling.

As they crouched, Niu had to rub his eyes between looking three times to his right along the parallel path leading into the stone terrace. How could this possibly be? he asked himself. What was a brightly colored, undulating, long-tailed dragon doing up here near the summit of the Langshan.

It was wending its way, slithering along with the motion of a ship upon a stormy sea, through the forest of pines, never seen in whole but in bits and pieces between the closely set trees of the pine copse. The dragon was snorting, and its undulating progress was what was being accompanied by the low drum beat and the playing of the flute. The dragon was twisting and turning and advancing upon the stone terrace in rhythm to the drum and flute.

And there was the beat of feet, many bare feet, and the humming of men—an almost human dragon. A sight to behold, one that Niu thought no one from the valley below, or in the markets of Nantung, would believe should he live to tell of what he saw and heard.

And when the dragon entered into the stone terrace and made a quick turn to the right, up the path toward the summit of the Langshan, Niu realized what it was. Nothing more than one of the ceremonial dragons that wended the streets of Nantung marking the Chinese New Year. A long, shiny-cloth costume, in brilliant yellows and blues and greens and white, slung over the bodies of many men, undulating around and twisting and turning, as it did through the streets of Nantung. In this case weaving around the summit of the Langshan, and now up, up, up toward the Dragon Temple, where, as the mists above them began to be burned off by the late morning sun, Niu could see what was perched at the very apex of the mountain. The Dragon Temple. White marble columns rising from pavilion platforms to high-peaked roofs covered with fish-scale shaped golden, vermillion, and emerald-colored tiles that gleamed in the bright sunshine like scales, there at the top of the world above the clouds separating the world of the monks from the common river valley dwellers.

And there, suspended from chain links high above his head, his cheek pressed into a marble column at the edge of one of the pavilion platforms, the rich folds lapping at his feet of the scarlet silk robe Niu had secretly given him when they had pledged to each other despite the rules of the nanleshijia, hung Niu's intended conquest and lover. Deming—naked and magnificent of body against the pristine backing of the mountaintop temple.

Shocked at the sight of his shackled erstwhile lover, Niu rose up onto his feet in the bed of ferns and opened his mouth to cry out to Deming. He was stopped, however, by the tug on his sleeve by the servant, Shun. Niu then remembered where he was and that it was death to be discovered there, and what he had started to call out to Deming stuck in his throat and came out as no more than a low gurgle.

Those of the dancing dragon did not hear Niu's cut-off exclamation or see him rise in the fern patch. They were turning their attention upward now, upward toward the new Dragon Temple initiate, the handsome, desirable Deming.

Niu collapsed back down into the bed of ferns and watched, in frustration and horror, as the undulating dragon, powered by a myriad of beefy, well-muscled, naked thighs wound and wove its way up the last flight of stone stairs to the base of the Dragon Temple monastery platforms, weaving its way, like an inevitable wave toward the ripe youth chained to the monastery pillar.

Niu let out a low, guttural moan as the dragon head reached Deming and reared up, revealing the naked body of the lead monk under the dragon covering. He embraced the shackled Deming from behind with one arm and wrapped the other around Deming's belly, pulling his hips back in presentation to a hard, thick, ready cock.

Niu nearly fainted back into Shun's arms with a sob, as he helplessly watched the first thrusting entrance of the initiation ceremony by the lead monk under the dancing dragon pelt between the thrust-back, plump buttocks cheeks of Deming, the one who Niu had been cultivating and saving for himself.

The baoan shuddered when Deming lifted his head and howled up into the heavens as he was taken for the first time in his initiation into the Dragon Temple community.

Spent within a short time, the lead monk, his head and upper torso still inside the dragon head, shook that head from side to side in obvious approval and ecstasy, pulled his spent *yang chu*—cock—out of Deming, and wove around to the side of him to provide place for the second set of legs under the dragon cloak to approach and the dragon cloth lift to reveal yet another young, vigorous, ready monk, who mounted Deming like a dog for the second taking. There were no fewer than seven more sets of legs covered by the dancing dragon, pounding up and down on the platform terrace, shuffling noisily to the sound of the drum and flute, anxiously waiting for their turn in the initiation of the new monk convert.

Niu found that he had collapsed back into Shun's arms. He was sobbing and shivering as he watched his well-laid plans being devoured by the lustful dragon. Deming was screaming out over the heightened sound of the flute and drum, but he must have been drugged or very well convinced that this was the life he wanted, because his cries were ones of joy and passion and encouragement—a lust for male attention that he'd never revealed to Deming with the same intensity he now was showing. His body writhed against the pillar as, one after another, the monks under the dragon covering approached him from the rear, revealed their well-toned and wanting bodies under the dragon cloak, lifted his hips in strong hands, and set his pelvis down on their eager, engorged cocks. With a howl of victory, each succeeding monk thrust a hard yang chu inside Deming's now gaping, flowing hole, and fucked him to their utter satiation.

Shun was humming and rocking Niu like a baby, doing all he could to sooth and calm the man he'd worshipped for many months but who had never so much as taken a glance at him, who had only had eyes for Deming.

As Niu watched Deming being taken time and time again, lustily, by strong, young, vigorous monks, and writhing away under the undulating dancing dragon, Niu became aware that he himself was aroused. His yang chu, his cock, was hard and throbbing. And he became aware, as he lay there in Shun's lap, being rocked and listening to Shun's low, soothing humming, that Shun's yang chu was hard too.

For the first time since he had become a baoan in the nanleshijia, Niu became aware of the servant Shun. He turned his face to Shun, took Shun's lips in his and kissed him deeply. In just the way he had imagined he would be doing with Deming.

Niu rolled to one side in the bed of ferns and scrabbled at his sash and opened his robe off of his body. Shun knelt in front of the baoan, his chosen master, took Niu's yang chu deep into his mouth, and made love to his cock, as Nui looked back up to the monastery platform. Deming was a mere rag doll now, exhausted and flopping around as yet another dragon-covered monk pumped his plump buttocks cheeks up and down on an angry-red, curved cock.

At length Niu could take no more, and he lifted Shun up and set him down in his lap, facing him, on his throbbing cock. Niu sighed and Shun groaned, as the warm, moist tightness of Shun descended slowly on Niu's throbbing yang chu. Niu sucked on Shun's hard nubs, while Shun used his strong calf and thigh muscles to ascend and descend on Niu's cock, sending the baoan into ever greater waves of paradise.

When the two were both spent, they turned their attention toward the monastery pavilions. Shun was still skewered in Niu's lap, both men enjoying the ebbing of Niu's manhood deep inside Shun, both savoring how they had moved as one and come as one, baoan and servant, but equal as lovers, if only temporarily.

The dancing dragon was gone now, and Deming was being unshackled by one of the monks, a hulking brute with a still-commanding cock jutting up and out of the center of him. The monk turned Deming, who just hung there, whimpering but with a big smile on his face, to his back against the pillar, lifted his torso with big beefy hands under his thighs, spread his legs and turned his pelvis up, and thrust his bulging cock up into him in a swift, deep piercing. Deming moaned and the monk grunted and groaned as he moved Deming's back up and down on the pillar by the power of his pistoning cock.

Both Niu and Shun felt life returning to the center of Niu at the observation of Deming's renewed taking, something that no longer bothered Niu in the least, and Shun turned in Niu's lap facing away from him and once more began rising and falling on Niu's rejuvenated yang chu, while Niu kissed him in the hollow of his neck, thumbed his hard nipples with one hand, and pumped on his young, hard cock with the other hand.

When all were finished this time, the monk left Deming in a heap on the silken scarlet hanfu—robe—Niu had provided him from what was now a long-ago and fading past.

"Do you want me to go and see if Deming wants to come back?" Shun asked in a low whisper. "Ask him whether he already has had enough of the world of the monks and wishes to leave?"

"No," Niu said, pulling himself away from Shun, donning his robe, and standing straight, once more taking command of his emotions and demeanor. "I wanted Deming only as a virgin. He is nothing to me now, and cannot return to the nanleshijia. Come. It's time for us to return there."

As Niu started limping back down the trail that descended Langshan, Shun, his channel aching from glorious use, struggled to keep within six paces of his chosen master. If desire for Deming could be thrust aside that easily, Shun wondered what use Niu would make of him now. Now that he'd had his desire fulfilled and been taken by the muscular brute, Shun wanted him all the more. But, while full of passion when they were fucking, Niu once more had erected a master-and-servant barrier between them. It was as if the taking had never happened.

Perhaps it is like that for Niu, thought Shun. But not for me. He will want me again someday, and then I will be in paradise again.

Chapter Three: Niu Serving the Duke of Shi

In the near distance, the lilting voice of Ping—Tranquility—supported by strums on his lute, set the mood in the summer pavilion, where the heat of the two young men added to the warm, humid breeze wafting down the Yangtze river and whispering up to the nanleshijia—the male pleasure house—setting the bamboo shoots screening the summer pavilion swaying and adding to the music of the lute.

"We must go no farther," jinan in training, Xiu, murmured in a small, hoarse voice. "No, you must not," he pleaded in a tone that regretted what it was duty-bound to say. "Oh, oh. ohhh."

"I must not do this?" the baoan—the nanleshijia protector—growled in a low, hoarse mutter. "And I must stop this?"

The young prostitute-in-training moaned a deep moan, his vermillion hanfu rustling, as he moved his hand inside the folds and clasped Niu's hand that had begun to move on his hardened cock.

"Your sweet yang chu is not telling me to cease, little one," Niu said, as he took one of Xiu's ears in his mouth and stuck his tongue in it. The young man shuddered and groaned. Niu began to match the rhythm of his tongue darting in and out of Xiu's ear with the hand stroking of the young man's cock. He placed his thumb on Xiu's bulb head and rubbed the slit there as he stroked. Xiu was trembling, and Niu knew the youth was his.

"I cannot be ruined," Xiu whispered forlornly.

"No one need ever know, not if we merely play suck the fruit," Niu said. "You have been trained right up to the act with a man's yang chu. Can you not tell that having done this, nothing can be detected?—not if you do not tell."

"I cannot," Xiu moaned. "The zhaoguzhe—the caretaker—would know. He would know."

"Not if you did not tell him. Neither would he know that you have permitted this," Niu muttered. He brushed aside the folds of Xiu's outer and inner robes and lifted the silk underskirt, exposing the young man's slim thighs and his hand-encased yang chu and pert little ball sack.

"He would know; he would know," Xiu was still murmuring. Then he gave a gasp as Niu's lips slid down the cylinder of his yang chu, replacing his hand as it, in turn, initially cupped Xiu's ball sack and then extended two fingers down along his perineum and back to the rim of the virginal ass channel.

Niu sucked hard on Xiu's bulb for a very few moments, with Xiu shuddering and giving little cries, before the young prostitute in training jerked three time and gave his seed up.

With his free hand, Niu unbound the sash of his own, more basic hanfu, and pushed it open. His throbbing manhood was in enormous erection. Xiu would have fainted to see it, but although Niu intended that the young man would feel it inside him, he felt there was no reason for Xiu to see it until after it had mastered him. He moved a hand back to Xiu's cock, which was already hardening again.

"He would not know. There is no reason anyone would know if you did not tell them," he was whispering. "You are no longer entirely pure now, anyway. You will do it so much better that first time for the man who pays for your virginity if you have already given it to me. I can teach you so much more of pleasing and being pleased by the yang chu than that old dried-up zhaoguzhe ever could."

"I cannot. Nothing can—"

"Nothing can?" Niu muttered, with a snort. "Then what are these twigs doing inside you? What is the difference between one thing inside you and another?" He moved the fingers that were now fully encased in the youth's channel so that Xiu could have no doubts he was fully possessed by them.

"Oh, ohhh," Xiu moaned. Xiu was moving his hips, back and forth, moving on Niu's fingers and in rhythm with the stroking of his cock. The campaign was complete, Niu realized with a secret smile. No matter with Xiu's lips said now, his body was Niu's. Nothing could stop Niu from adding another virgin to his collection.

"They pleasure you, do they not? My yang chu will equally pleasure you in their stead."

Niu knew the pleasure part would be real for the young man—when he was fully saddled and possessed—but he also knew that having his yang chu inside the youth was nothing like just these two fingers, no matter how plump they were.

Xiu looked at Niu plaintively.

"Do you want me?" Niu asked, knowing full well what the answer was. He had slowly prepared Xiu for this for months. "And do you trust me that we can pleasure ourselves and the zhaoguzhe will never know?"

Xiu did not answer, but he did not struggle either. Niu placed the palm of a hand in the young man's sternum and gently pressed him back onto the pillows deeply piled on the summer pavilion platform.

The youth was whimpering and Niu could feel the trembling going through the young man's body as he grasped Xiu's legs and parted and raised them, twisted his own body around, and came up on his knees between the young man's thighs.

What did he want? What was his goal beyond burying his yang chu deep inside this beautiful young man, splitting

27

him, and making him quiver in the losing of his virginity? Niu had not thought beyond achieving the forbidden. Did he want to hold back until the jinan begged for it, or did he want to ruin him? Did Niu want to stay in a position he despised in the nanleshijia, which would mean that he would have to help Xiu cover up his deflowering? Or did he want to brutalize the so-sweet young channel and then strike off on his own?

He moved the bulbous cap of his club to the trembling rim of the besotted, trusting young courtesan to be, still undecided whether to thrust or to work his way in gently. All he had known was that he wanted to collect as many virgin deflowerings in his life as he could as long as his virility was at its peak.

As he was about to close his mind down and let his body do what it wished to do, the tinkling of the bells along the pathway from the main house to the summer pavilion, set off by the movement of the robe hems of the walker, performed the task they were meant to do—to give warning of an approaching figure.

Niu barely had time to jump up from the pillows and tie his sash and move to attention near the entrance arbor and for Xiu to likewise readjust his hanfu and lay back in the pillows and close his eyes as if taking a sleep, when the zhaoguzhe—the caretaker—swept into the pavilion. He cast a suspicious look at both the jinan in preparation and the baoan, but, not being able to discern that anything was amiss, turned and spoke to Niu gruffly.

"You are to come with me, baoan."

"We . . . I have only arrived. Xiu was missing from the main pavilion and I came looking for him."

The zhaoguzhe looked at Niu with increased suspicion. It can be folly to give too much of an excuse where none was requested. Be that as it may, though, this particular problem was already solved.

"You are to come with me because you are leaving the nanleshijia," the caretaker said in a near growl.

"Leaving?"

"Yes. You expressed a wish—an ambition—some time ago, and I have remembered and have made it so."

"An ambition?"

"Yes. I have sold you to the Duke of Shi. You are to enter military service with him in Yangzhou. You stated your wish to become a warrior. So a warrior you will become."

"Yangzhou? The Duke of Shi?" Niu was bewildered, but his voice was joyous and a broad grin spread across his face.

Hearing the effect that the news had on Niu, Xiu slitted his eyes open and a involuntary look of despair spread across his own face.

This was not lost on the zhaoguzhe, who now hoped that he had been in time to divert disaster.

* * * *

The four guards pressed in close to Niu on all sides as they climbed the circling stone stairs up and up into the tower of the Duke of Shi's castle in Yangzhou, the seat of Nanfeng, the prefecture Nantung was in. Niu had never been this high from the ground before—not even when he was a youth and climbed trees to look down on the world and imagine that everything he could see was his.

He didn't know why he had been roughly awakened before dawn and marched through the castle. He had trained well as a warrior. He knew he'd done so. And he could tell that the Duke of Shi was pleased, as he had watched Niu closely in the training sessions.

Next to Niu himself, the duke was the tallest and most muscular figure on the training ground. His commanding presence and fierce attitude could not be ignored. Niu knew that if and when they went to battle, the duke would stand his ground and would be in the forefront of battle. He would make the enemy melt away from him simply by drawing himself up to his full, magnificent stature and glowering at the enemy.

He was a man who always got his way. Of that Niu was sure.

Perhaps he had shown too much interest in Niu, the former baoan thought. Niu thought that the nanleshijia was rife with intrigue and scheming, but it had been nothing there like it was here at the center of power of one of the Wu kingdom's foremost prefectures. Perhaps others, jealous that the duke could show favor to Niu, were doing something to take Niu out of the equation.

But this proved not to be the case.

When Niu and his escorts reached the room at the top of the tower, he found the duke himself, in hanfu—robes—of royal blue, reclining against pillows with a tea table set in front of him. This tableau was set up in the middle of the round chamber. The only other furniture in the room was a substantial cot piled high with animal skins, four torches set at intervals around on the stone walls, a piss pot against the wall near the bed, and a frame contraption across the room from the bed, which seemed to be some sort of high-raised chair, with the leather hide of a cow slung between the corners of the frame. There were four slit windows set at intervals around the walls that were too narrow for a man to get his head through.

"Niu. Thank you for coming to see me," the duke said in a calm, even voice.

Niu almost laughed, knowing that he had been brought here by no choice of his own.

"Come. Come, sit with me. No, not across from me. Here, beside me."

When Niu had tentatively knelt down beside where the duke sat in the pillows, the duke leaned over the table and poured tea into a cup and offered it to Niu.

Niu carefully took the cup, almost overwhelmed by the honor that was being bestowed on him by this gesture.

"Shall we become more comfortable?" the duke murmured, giving Niu a smile. He reached over then and untied Niu's sash and parted the young man's hanfu. Having barely had time to leave his bed when summoned, Niu was naked underneath.

"I see that our military training has toughened you up nicely," the duke murmured.

Niu moved instinctively to pull his hanfu closed again, but two guards were at his back in a flash, growling, and letting him know that he had overstepped his bounds.

"Let us not forget that you are in my service, Niu. That I own you." At a signal from the duke, the other two guards stepped to his side, one leaned over and untied his sash, and the other slowly pulled the robes off the duke's shoulders, revealing a massive, barrel chest that was heavily marked with healed wounds and slash marks.

"Feel these, Niu. These are marks of honor." He took one of Niu's hands in his. At first Niu resisted but at a growl and the pressure of hands on his naked shoulders, he relaxed and let the duke take his fingers to the marks on his chest and trace the wounds.

"I have watched you in training, Niu. You are worthy to be in my guard—my own bodyguard."

"Thank you, sire," Niu murmured, knowing the honor this was and not knowing what else to say. His mind was racing on the situation he was in, though. What was expected of him; where was this headed?

"My guards must be completely loyal, Niu. They must desire nothing more than what I desire; they must dedicate themselves to me completely."

The duke was moving Niu's hand down his torso, into the folds of robing gathered around his waist. His yang chu was hard as a rock and in full erection.

"Show me that you are prepared to fully serve me, Niu," the duke whispered, his voice thick with arousal. His hand was encasing Niu's hand, which was encasing the duke's cock.

"Sire," Niu murmured.

"You pleasure yang chu's in your throat, Niu. I know that you do. The soldiers tell me that you have done that here. You have, I believe, ruined every virgin male in my guard."

I prepare them and then I fuck them, yes, Niu thought. Is that what the duke wants me to do? To pleasure his yang chu and then to ride his noble ass?

One of the guards was pushing Niu's face down into the duke's lap, while the other one knelt beside Niu and swallowed Niu's cock and began to work it.

Niu gave the duke suck, and the duke sighed and reclined back on the pillows. As was Niu's technique, he began

31

working a hand between the duke's thighs after giving his ball sack into play. But before his fingers could reach the duke's rim, the warrior growled and guards were right there, slapping Niu's hand away and trapping his arms behind his back.

Niu realized now that it was not meant for him to be fucking the duke, although someone here would be fucked. He began to struggle against those holding him in thrall, but it was no use.

At the duke's direction, the four guards manhandled Niu up from the pillows and hauled him over to the seat-like contraption. They thrust him into a seated position in the sling and held his arms and legs down.

The duke rose from the pillows, shrugging his robes completely off his body. He turned, facing Niu. His erection was enormous, both longer and thicker than Niu's own, which itself was one of the most magnificent in Nantung. He no longer was in Nantung, though. In Nantung, he was the taker; no one had dared to try to top him.

The duke smiled a wicked smile and was stroking his cock, as he slowly approached the sling contraption. As he moved between Niu's legs, Niu cried out, "I yield to no man!"

But, with a strong thrust inside Niu that made him howl, the duke growled, "I am no man. I am the Duke of Shi. And all who serve me are prepared to serve me fully."

Niu struggled mightily, but the four strong soldiers held him fast as the duke had his way with him.

When he had come, he pulled out of Niu and said, "Very nice. You will do nicely. And as you service me, likewise you serve my four captains."

As the four soldiers, each in turn, fucked Niu as well, the duke moved back to the pillows and tea table, gathered his hanfu about him, reclined, and watched the takings with a smile.

When the fourth soldier was finished, Niu lay there in the sling chair, spent in body, but still defiant in mind.

Sensing this, the duke stood and said, "I like your spirit. But if you leave this room alive it will be in willing service to me. I leave you to think it over. When I come through that

32

door again, you will beg for the yang chu if you have decided to serve me."

Niu looked upon the departing duke with dull eyes. He was prepared to fight at the man's side, but he was no one's woman.

The next night, the duke arrived—this time with six rather than four guards. Niu was as defiant. And Niu was taken seven times.

On the second night, the duke and eight guards were met at the door by a groveling Niu, who knelt at the duke's feet and begged to be taken, pledging devoted service to his master.

They fucked on the cot this time, with the guards watching but not needing to hold Niu down. Niu raised his bare buttocks to the duke and spread his own cheeks as the duke worked inside him. He also met each thrust of the duke's with a backward thrust of his own hips and cried out for the fuck, asking for more each time the duke was spent—and then receiving more when the duke was recovered.

The third night, Niu was returned to the barracks to sleep with the other warriors of the duke's bodyguard.

On the fourth night, when the nightly count was taken in the barracks, Niu was missing.

* * * *

Shun was standing next to the shower stall at the nanleshijia, eyes downcast, holding Xiu's hanfu—robes—when he felt the strong pressure on his arm and looked up and into the eyes of the former baoan, Niu.

He's come back for me, was Shun's first thought, but then he saw that Niu was looking beyond him, to the shower stall, where Xiu stood under the cascade of water. The perfectly formed white orbs of his buttocks could be seen protruding beyond the side wall of the shower stall.

Niu gave Shun a meaningful look, and casting his eyes down again so that the former baoan couldn't see the pain and longing in them, Shun let the hanfu fall to the stone terrace and backed away.

Niu moved silently to the stall and came in close behind the young Xiu. He raised his hand to the one Xiu was using to pull on the chain loosing the water above his head, and, releasing the chain, Xiu gave a little gasp.

He turned his head, and his lips were met with those of Niu, which were brutal and demanding, demanding entrance. Xiu yielded his lips and the inner reaches of his mouth to the possessing lips and tongue of the man who would be his lover but who had deserted him for the life of a warrior.

Niu encircled the young jinan with his arms and covered Xiu's pectorals with his rough hands, evoking groans and grunts from the young man as his thumbs and forefingers worried Xiu's nipples.

Withdrawing from the kiss, Niu whispered in Xiu's ear, "I could not stand not having you. I will take you now."

"*Shih, shih, shih.* Yes, yes, yes," Xiu hissed. "Now."

Niu ran one hand down Xiu's torso to his belly and palmed him there. His other hand went to Xiu's buttocks, which he stroked lovingly. Xiu arched his back and thrust his buttocks into Niu's midsection, trembling as he felt the need of Niu for him through the material of the former baoan's robes.

"Now, now," Xiu muttered with a sigh. "I beg you. Don't make me wait." His hands went to his own buttocks, pulling the orbs apart, preparing for the mounting.

Niu's hand was moving inside the folds of his hanfu to free his cock, when his movement was arrested by the grip of a hand on his arm.

"If you wish to live, you will be gone now." The zhaoguzhe's eyes flashed with anger.

"I will have what I came for first," Niu growled.

"I know you have escaped from the duke's service. Everyone in Nantung knows. The duke's men are approaching. If you don't leave right this moment, we will all be seeing your head on a pike above the town gate at dawn."

Niu flashed the caretaker a look of hatred, but he unhanded Xiu, who collapsed with a sob to the floor of the shower stall, and backed away. Looking wildly around, his eyes lit on Shun who had returned to the circle of light.

"I know how you can escape," Shun said with an excited voice. "I will show you, if you will take me with you."

The two were gone in a flash, leaving the zhaoguzhe standing over the naked huddled figure on the shower stall floor. He raised a hand over his head. In it he was clutching the strip of leather he'd brought out to the shower stall in a rush as soon as he heard that Niu was back. It was a thick strip of leather, designed to sting but to leave a mark for only a few days. When he brought his hand down smartly, Xiu cried out and flinched at the sting of the leather strip on his bare flesh. But he remained folded inside himself, not thinking of being switched again and again and again but of what he had precipitously lost for a second time.

Chapter Four: The Short Career Life of a Bitten Peach Trouper

Xiaodan—Little Dawn—had known it was coming— more or less. Less, as it inevitably turned out. He just didn't fully know what "it" was. His parents, no his whole village, had been honored when, as a particularly small and well-formed and fair-of-face child, he had been taken from his parents at a young age and sent to the renowned nanleshijia in Nantung. From the beginning of his two years there, he had been told he was very special. But still he was surprised when, barely into his training as a jinan—a male courtesan—and two years short of reaching his majority, he was selected to train for the King of Wu's Golden Peach troupe, a very special troupe of actors who only performed for a very select group at the Imperial Court in the kingdom's capital city of Gusu. He was told this was a great honor, and he of course believed the house's caretaker, the zhaoguzhe, when he was assured of this.

After being taken from the nanleshijia in a palanquin sent by the court at Gusu, Xiaodan was transported to the capital city and trained for two years more in playing the female parts in the troupe's highly refined and specialized dramas shown only in the Imperial Court and only at the pleasure and invitation of the King of Wu.

He had now learned all there was to know of the dress and of the walk and of the positioning of hands—and of the facial expressions that went with each of the traditional symbols of the time-honored stage scenarios. He learned to smile demurely and look away in embarrassment, he learned to slit his eyes and wet his lips with his tongue, and he learned to open his mouth wide and lift his eyes to the heaven—and even how to swoon in this, the wu, or fifth, movement of the basic play form he was being taught. He practiced the sounds the female characters made—the sigh, and the little giggle, and the long moan. And he learned to dress. The special robe of heavy brocade, cinched with the tight, breath-taking sash. The two-sectioned white sock slippers and the wooden platform sandals that gave the Chinese imperial female her peculiar gait. He at first had thought it strange there were no foundation garments, but he was told that the brocade was so heavy that to wear too much during a performance would cause him to sweat and his white pancake makeup to run.

He was taught all of the expressions and movements and sounds he was to make in the female role in Golden Peach productions. But he only learned these in theory and in solitary practice with his tutors. He had never practiced with any of the other actors of the troupe—indeed he never had met any of them. He himself was not privileged to watch a Golden Peach performance. They were so special that they were meant for the eyes of only a few.

He had begged Hsiang, the troupe master, to declare him ready to perform—he had perfected everything.

"And have you perfected the knowledge that you represent your parents, your very ancestors, and your village in this role and that how you deport yourself, how well you stay within your role, no matter what, will determine either the reward or punishment of everyone you know down two generations?"

"Yes, yes, Laoshi," Xiaodan answered, using the revered words for master teacher for the one man who controlled not only his destiny but that of his entire village and extended family.

"Then I will look for a time when you can perform your first play. You must perform that well, with no deviation from role, and you must fully satisfy your audience, or you will have failed. And you understand what failure means, don't you?"

"Yes, Laoshi." He knew this was a serious point, as Master Hsiang kept returning to it. Of course he would do well; he had trained for this female role in the imperial dramas for years. "And what play will I be performing, Laoshi? I must practice that one especially hard."

"Always the first Golden Peach troupe play for the female role is 'First Bite.' I presume you know that one well."

"Yes, yes, of course," Xiaodan said. He knew the play, but it was one of the sadder ones. It was a play where two actors are playing opposite the female role on the platform outside a pavilion in the jade garden at night, while the breeze whispers through the maple trees surrounding the koi pond and singsong girls play on the lute and sing sad songs behind the diaphanous curtains of the pavilion. One man tells the female a sad story of a fallen family, shown in the images on a scroll he shows her while weaving his story. She is sitting very close to him and feels overheated by the warm night air and by the sadness of the images depicted as the chronology of the scroll unwinds. She moans her sadness and her faintness from the close air, and the two men console her.

It was a mournful tale, and the older, long-past retired female role actor who had taught the role to Xiaodan had told it with emotion and trembling hands.

At last it was the day of the performance. Xiaodan was primped and trimmed throughout the day—bathed thrice in highly scented baths, and all of his bodily hair except that on his head plucked away. He was told that nothing could impede the smooth rustling of the brocade on his body as he went through his highly stylized movements. Two hours before the performance he was given a potion in strong wine. This was to make him slightly faint to aid in the realism of playing out this highly important, crucially significant first performance. This too he had practiced for this play before, so it came as no surprise to him.

When he was bid to flutter out onto the stage, and to move toward the two men seated behind a low tea table on large, raised pillows, the setting was just as Xiaodan had imagined it would be—everything was just where it was supposed to be. The table and cushions were set out on a polished-wood platform beside a koi pond and under a full moon. A slight breeze was rustling through the maple trees. Soft light filtered out to encompass the area of the tea table from a curtained pavilion. The front section of the pavilion, toward the stage, was open to the platform. Five men, in magnificent silken hanfu—robes—with many different-colored layers of undergarments, were artfully settled on cushions in a ring around the covered pavilion section, all facing the stage area. They each had a low table beside them on which various drinks and delicacies for the palate were positioned, and they had cushions they could lean back on as they watched the play. Kneeling beside each was a young, handsome youth, none much older than Xiaodan, who were dressed only in diaphanous billowy trousers held up with a golden waist chain. Silken panels of cloth, each of a different color, were tucked into the waist chain front and back to clothe their privates.

Somewhere in the curtained-off portion of the pavilion behind where the dignitaries were lounging were the singsong girls, playing their lutes and singing their sad songs in soft, whispery tones.

The two actors Xiaodan minced toward, in studied, slow movements, on his precariously high wooden platform sandals, were quite different from one another. And, to Xiaodan's surprise they did not wear the white pancake makeup that had been carefully applied to his face in the forming of his countenance into the epitome of female beauty before the black stiff-haired wig was set on his head.

The one actor, who was holding the partially unrolled scroll out in front of him was fairly young and was robust looking. He was wearing a shiny black hanfu of trim cut, and his arms were bare, showing heavily muscled biceps and forearms and the intricate lacing of black tattoos in the design of a spider web. He had the face of a seasoned warrior, and Xiaodan would have guessed he was an acrobat and decided to think of him as such.

The other actor was elderly, with stark white hair and a long, wispy beard. He was heavier than the first man, but not exactly fat. But of the two, he was the one who commanded attention. His hanfu was deep purple in color, which identified him to anyone in the land as imperial, not more than two removes from the sitting king. Xiaodan gasped at being in the presence of someone like him. Could it possibly be that a member of the imperial family acted with the Golden Peach troupe? Perhaps that was why Xiaodan had not been told of the other actors, he thought. Was he in the presence of something far greater than he had ever imagined? Even if he had not been wearing purple, Xiaodan would have known this man was the most commanding figure anywhere in the vicinity. He was obviously a warrior of old, proven by a slashed cut on his face that went from ear to chin and that was only partially hidden by the wisps of his white beard. Indeed, Xiaodan got the impression that the imperial elder didn't want the cut to be hidden. The slash had caught the corner of an eye too, and that eye drooped a bit, certainly more than the other one.

But those eyes caught Xiaodan's attention. The old man was watching him intently as he minced across the platform, and a shiver ran down Xiaodan's spine. He didn't know what the stare meant, but he felt like he was being eaten alive. And Xiaodan continued to be confused that the imperial elder was there at all. This was the stage; this was a Golden Peach performance. Upon even the slight reflection he was permitted, Xiaodan could not believe that this imperial elder was one of the actors. Why wasn't the elder watching from the pavilion?

The younger, dark actor, the acrobat, motioned for Xiaodan to sit on the cushion between him and the older actor, and, as if on cue, the music rose in volume from behind curtain at the back of the pavilion.

Looking back over at the elder actor, Xiaodan noticed that there was yet another youth there, like the ones kneeling near the dignitaries in the pavilion. He had been hidden behind the billowing purple hanfu—robes—of the elder.

As woozy as Xiaodan was from the potion he had been given, one that made him feel loose through his body, Xiaodan fought hard to maintain his role. The acrobat was starting his melodious recitation of the story of the scroll that now was unrolling from one side and being rolled back up from the other side immediately in front of Xiaodan's eyes, and he immediately went into shock. The acrobat had an arm around Xiaodan's waist on the side from which the chronology of the scroll was appearing. This was all according to the play. Xiaodan was playing the female role. He was supposed to be emotional and to begin to tremble and give little gasps.

That Xiaodan didn't really have to act this out but had had it drilled into him so deeply that he was naturally living the role he was trained to didn't prevent him being shocked by what he was being forced to see.

It wasn't just the story of one family's tragedies. It wasn't a Chinese scroll at all. It was a scroll of a Japanese art Xiaodan had only heard about in passing, behind twittering fingers, spoken in the dark of night and only between young friends who were taking risks and practicing coming of age far earlier than custom dictated. These were Shunga images, the pillow images of the Japanese underworld. And not just any Shunga images. These were images of men in exotic sex positions with each other. And the yang chu on the controlling men were of gigantic proportions.

Xiaodan felt like he might swoon. Which very interesting, because this was exactly where he was supposed to half swoon in the play script. He was also supposed to let out a little moan, which he did on cue—without needing the cue.

And then also on cue, the younger, dark actor set the scroll down on the table and lifted Xiaodan onto his lap. He enfolded Xiaodan inside his arms and picked up the scroll and began to roll through the increasingly suggestive images again. The images of the sexual positions were becoming more and more explicit. Less and less clothing was in view. The sexual act was progressing further, the takers in the images becoming bolder, more insistent, their yang chu monstrous.

41

Xiaodan groaned and looked away from the scroll, just as he was trained to do at this point. And the acrobat encasing him lifted a hand, took hold of Xiaodan's chin, and forced his eyes back on the scroll. The scroll had reached a point where a smaller man, completely naked, was being held to the front of a larger, heavily muscled, fully tattooed man's middle, as the larger man paraded around in a circle. Xiaodan could see what was transpiring, as the half-buried phallus of the larger man could be seen up the hole of the younger one. The smaller man was in a swoon, his clothing and once-perfectly coiffured hair in dishabille.

Xiaodan gasped, just as he was supposed to at this point. His gasp was involuntary, though, because he suddenly could feel the strength of the other actor's manhood beneath him through the one layer of brocade he wore. His yang chu was enormous. This wasn't in the script, but the partial faint that followed it was. And, as in the script, Xiaodan came around shortly with the strong scent of a reviving potion under his nose, being held by the acrobat. The actor's other hand, however, had entered the folds of Xiaodan's hanfu and found and encircled his member.

Xiaodan gasped again and moaned and groaned, just as he had been taught to do at this point in the play. He was no longer being forced to look at the scroll, because the actor's two hands were now engaged in other activities. The one was teasing Xiaodan's cock to erection and the other had slipped in above the sash and was pinching at one of Xiaodan's nipples. Xiaodan was also being moved around in languid circles on the actor's lap, and the actor's member was much more evident and much more in play between the crease that separated Xiaodan's slim moons.

Xiaodan looked around wildly for escape or help. Strangely enough this action fell right into play with the script of the "First Bite," and Xiaodan was beginning to more fully understand what he had learned—and why.

The elder was still sitting there close to him, his eyes boring into Xiaodan, drinking in each violation Xiaodan was experiencing. But now there was a bobbing head in his lap. The young attendant who had once been behind him now had lowered his face and both of his hands into the imperial elder's lap, the hanfu spread just enough to give the attendant entrance. Xiaodan could see the pink skin of a long phallus that was largely flaccid but that was showing some signs of hardening. The elder was breathing heavily, and he had a heavily ringed hand on the back of the young attendant's head, but his eyes were still drinking in Xiaodan, savoring every awakening of Xiaodan's senses and realization.

Xiaodan looked wildly out to the audience of five for some sign of succor and reason, but each of the five now was already in some stage of being sucked by his personal attendant or in full-blown servicing, having easily pulled away the colorful loin cloths and gained quick entry to their attendant's privates. The attendants were in various forms of compliance. The two attending the dignitaries in the middle had begun riding the cocks of their assigned master already, both barely started in taking in the poles they were riding, and were leaning in toward each other and kissing and running hands along hard, aroused flesh. Two others were still giving suck. The fifth was being ravished, almost as if against his will. He was crying out loudly, which could have something to do with his very small size and the very large cock that was pushing into him as he was half kneeling in the cushions and having his face pushed down by a large hand while his tormenter crouched behind him.

All but this fifth dignitary were still watching Xiaodan, though, interested in following the first bite into that peach. And except for the one who had lost control, the impression was given that they were gauging themselves to the rise and release of the imperial elder.

About the time that Xiaodan thought that the actor manhandling him was going to sweep the thin layers of brocade between their bodies away and bite the peach himself, the attendant servicing the imperial elder lifted his head in triumph to reveal a long, strong cock rising out of the folds of his master's hanfu.

The attendant drew away as the actor holding Xiaodan stood, bringing Xiaodan with him, and took two steps toward the imperial elder and lowered Xiaodan's moons into his lap.

The attendant held the root of the old man's cock straight up and made sure his bulb aligned with Xiaodan's hole. Then the acrobat actor and the younger attendant each was holding one of Xiaodan's thighs out wide and had laced their other arms around Xiaodan's back and were pressing him down onto the imperial elder's phallus with hands on his shoulders.

Xiaodan was beyond the script now and wailing his pain and taking for all to hear. The music had stopped. All of the fucking stopped in the pavilion except for that of the dignitary who had lost complete control of himself, and he was quickly swept out of the scene by two burly soldiers, probably never to be invited to a special Golden Peach performance again, possibly never even to be seen anywhere again.

For several minutes the attendant and the acrobat slowly pumped Xiaodan up and down on the imperial elder's member as it dug deeper inside the virginal territory. The imperial elder hummed and grunted in appreciation, and Xiaodan, remembering at last that this was a performance being assessed against the very existence of his family and village, subsided into sobs interlaced as he was able with sighs and moans of enjoyment and admiration for the imperial elder to benefit from.

Xiaodan had lost his wig when the acrobat had raised him off of the cushions, and now he was being stripped of his robe as well. The imperial elder having gained purchase deep inside him, the attendant let loose of Xiaodan and knelt in front of him and gave him suck until Xiaodan jerked and released his seed. The other actor took possession of Xiaodan's lips. Both of these attendants were doing what they could to help Xiaodan make the best impression he could on the old man. Proving that he hadn't lost his strength, the elder was holding the diminutive Xiaodan by the waist with two gnarled but strong hands and was now pulling the young actor up and down on his gloriously rejuvenated, if only for a short time, member.

With a cry of victory, the imperial elder came inside the virginal offering in two weak, but not-to-be-taken-for-granted spurts. The four remaining dignitaries also gave a restrained cheer of approval and returned to their fucking. Now they were free to ejaculate as well. And now the attendants were groaning under the fully self-centered rutting of the aroused dignitaries.

The Imperial elder waved his hand and the young actor shed his black hanfu, revealing his body to be that of the magnificent acrobat Xiaodan had thought he might be. He was covered nearly shoulder to ankle in intricate black-ink tattoo lacing, and he had a magnificently thick and long—and fully engorged—cock.

As the elder's attendant moved in close so that the elder could wrap an arm around his waist and undo his loin cloth and begin to suck the young man's cock while pulling hopefully on his own now-diminished member, the acrobat picked a swooning Xiaodan up, turned him to face the dignitaries, crouched his knees slightly, and slammed the newly bitten peach down hard onto his cock. Xiaodan flung his appendages out wide and cried to the full moon at the rough slide of the cock, much longer and thicker than the one that had taken the first bite, and he just flopped around like a rag doll, skewered solidly to the acrobat's pelvis as the actor marched around the platform and jostled his newfound friend up and down on his virile member.

Xiaodan recalled in horror that this was precisely the last image he had seen on the forbidden scroll. He was only reminded of this though, because in his last pass by the low table, the acrobat took up the scroll and tossed it to the dignitaries, all of whom were now finished with their first taking and ready for more entertainment from the platform.

The four dignitaries huddled over the scroll and sang out sexual taking positions they were interested in seeing, and the muscled acrobat, the real center and star of the Golden Peach troupe, showed that he could perform each position with the now completely limp and compliant Xiaodan.

Later, much later, when Hsiang and the troupe's attendants were sponging off Xiaodan's bruised body and the young man had come around to the smell of vinegar under his nose, he asked if he had satisfied and where his acting career went from here.

"Yes, you were very satisfactory," Hsiang whispered in a lulling tone. "Your family and village will be richly rewarded. It is increasingly difficult to satisfy the king's brother. He was well satisfied with what you drew out of him."

"But as for a stage career," he continued in a sad voice, "I'm afraid that was your premier and last performance with the Golden Peach troupe. You cannot take two bites out of that peach."

"But what will happen to me?" wailed Xiaodan.

"You will return to Nantung, to the Cut Sleeve Nanleshijia from which you came to us."

"But the zhaoguzhe told me I was not being trained to be a jinan—a male prostitute," Xiaodan exclaimed in despair.

"And you shall not be," Hsiang said with a satisfied laugh. "You have been deflowered by the brother of the King of Wu. You will be no mere jinan. You will be a courtesan now and will be engaged by only the richest and most refined men of the Yangzhou prefecture."

Xiaodan wasn't sure he fully appreciated that there was a difference of any significance between a jinan and a male courtesan.

* * * *

When he returned to Nantung, Xiaodan was assigned a room all his own and prepared for his new life. He was already more highly trained in the arts of the actor—of pleasing men in foreplay—than the other jinan in the house.

"You have not been fully prepared for the one who has bought your exclusive contract," the zhaoguzhe—caretaker of the Cut Sleeve Nanleshijia—told him. And as Xiaodan watched his master with wide eyes, too shy to tell him of the monster phallus of the acrobat at court, the zhaoguzhe brought forth a collection of phalluses, of graduated sizes.

"You will appreciate that we have prepared you in this way," the zhaoguzhe said when he had slipped one of the smaller-sized phalluses into Xiaodan's channel and tied it fast around his waist.

In two weeks, as Xiaodan was lounging in the main pavilion with the other jinan and listening to Ping sing and play his lute, the zhaoguzhe entered and beckoned to Xiaodan.

"It is time," was all he said.

They walked slowly down the passageway to Xiaodan's private chamber, with the zhaoguzhe hissing admonishments and whispering directions while they were en route. He was flustered and sweating, and Xiaodan decided that the man they were going to see must be very important indeed, and he too began to tremble.

"You have been honored. Your patron is none other than the Duke of Shi."

And then they were at the door. Xiaodan entered and the caretaker backed away, leaving him alone with three men in the room. Two of them where hulking bodyguards standing at near attention in the far corner of his room. The third, a monstrously large and heavily muscled man in an imperial blue hanfu, was sitting on pillows behind a low tea table in the center of the room.

"Xiaodan. Thank you for coming to see me," the duke said in a calm, even voice. "I am told that your virginity was taken by the prince brother of the King of Wu and that you have known the yang chu of no other man since that day."

"Yes, that is true," Xiaodan said with downcast eyes. It was technically true. The acrobat had taken him but it was on the same day as the prince took his virginity.

"That is quite an honor for you—and signifies the patrons of the House of Wu expect to sponsor you for the remainder of your youth. You must feel privileged."

"Yes, of course."

"Come. Come, sit with me. No, not across from me. Here, beside me."

When Xiaodan had tentatively knelt down beside where the duke sat in the pillows, the duke leaned over the table and poured tea in a cup and offered it to Xiaodan.

Xiaodan carefully took the cup, almost overwhelmed by the honor that was being bestowed on him by this gesture.

"Shall we become more comfortable?" the duke murmured, giving Xiaodan a smile. He reached over then and

47

untied Xiaodan's sash and parted the young man's hanfu. Xiaodan was naked underneath. Feigning modesty, Xiaodan moved instinctively to pull his hanfu closed again, but the duke brushed his hands away and moved his own hands inside the folds of Xiaodan's hanfu.

Xiaodan sighed and gave a little moan that he knew would please the duke. He was trembling, but this was no act. The duke was huge of stature and his massive yang chu was peeking out of the folds of his hanfu.

"Tell me, sweet Xiaodan. Did you take the prince brother's withered yang chu in your mouth?"

"No, sire, I did not," Xiaodan answered.

"So in that, at least, I will be the first," the duke said, and putting his hands on the back of Xiaodan's head, he guided the young courtesan's mouth down to the waiting cock. Xiaodan's jaw was unhinged in taking the staff in and he gagged on the massiveness of it, but he had been trained to do this with fruit, and he managed artfully, bringing the heavily breathing duke near to climax. The duke pushed his away, though, and sat there, staring hard at the young courtesan as he regained his composure.

"On your knees and forearms as a dog of the alley," the duke whispered in a deep voice at length.

"Sire?" Xiaodan said, with surprise.

The duke lifted the body of the courtesan and pushed him down on his hands and knees. "Like a dog of the alley," he said. "The leavings of the House of Wu, the oppressors of my family for centuries."

Xiaodan shuddered and attempted to rise, but already the duke was astride his hips, trapping Xiaodan's buttocks between his strong thighs. He thrust inside the courtesan's channel, and Xiaodan cried out in pain and surprise at the lack of preparation and foreplay. He would have thanked the zhaoguzhe for the weeks of preparation of his channel for a monster's cock, but the zhaoguzhe had misjudged the Duke of Shi.

The duke grabbed a handful of Xiaodan's head hair and arched the young courtesan's back toward him and started pumping hard and deep.

Xiaodan's cries of pain and violation slowly changed to passion and ecstasy as his channel was mined deeper and spread wider than ever before. The man was a brute but he was a god of stamina and of taking a man as he'd never been taken before. Xiaodan came again and again, but the duke fucked on. The passion phase moved to exhaustion and begging for mercy, mercy that never came. And when the duke did come it was deep inside Xiaodan with boiling fury and a flood of cum that burbled out of Xiaodan's channel and down his thighs.

When he was finished, Xiaodan's bruised body slumped to the floor. The two guards stepped forward and helped the duke don and adjust his hanfu again.

"He is sweet, but he has been with the House of Wu. We will take him with us. You may take him straight to the barracks and all of the soldiers may enjoy him as they will."

"And then bring him back to you?" One of the guards asked.

"No, you may keep him in the barracks as long as he lasts."

They did not leave at once, however. The duke sat back at his tea table and watched as the two bodyguards had Xiaodan as well—together. Xiaodan lay between them, nearly comatose, his tongue hanging out and panting lightly and his eyes staring blindly at the ceiling corners of the room he never again would see.

After that Xiaodan was taken away from the Cut Sleeve Nanleshijia to disappear into the confines of the duke's castle in Yangzhou, never to be heard from again.

Chapter Five: Niu and the King of Wu

They were camped near the top of the ridge in a meadow, just below the forest line. Niu had said he wanted to be high up whenever he could. He was standing there looking out over the thousands of cook fires and tents spread across the meadow when Shun, carrying the supplies for both of them, managed to trudge up the hillside from the road below.

"I wonder which one he is in?" Niu said to no one in particular.

"Who?" Shun murmured as he prepared to set up their encampment.

"The king. The King of Wu. Jili. He must be down there somewhere."

Shun clucked his lips. He'd heard this a thousand times on their journey from Nantung, first to the Wu capital of Gusu, only to learn that the king was on the march into the neighboring kingdom to the north, Chu, to redress some grievance of his own—or of his own devising. He was known to be fierce for war—not necessarily to acquire land and booty but just because he enjoyed it and wanted to keep his army on a fine edge of preparedness.

Since they had left Nantung in the middle of the night just ahead of the Duke of Shi's avenging guard, though, Niu had had the obsession to join with Jili and to swear allegiance to him. The servant Shun had the impression that he wanted to do so because the king and the duke were sworn enemies. Niu had been taken into the service of the duke from the Nantung nanleshijia—male pleasure house—that they had both been employed in. But Niu had returned soon thereafter, pledging enmity for the duke for some indignity he would not name and with the duke's soldiers in hot pursuit.

Niu now was seeking out the King of Wu, and, nonsensically, Shun thought, assumed that he could audience with the king directly. He apparently believed that all he would need do was meet directly with the king and a collaboration would be struck.

Shun half believed that this could be done. Niu was an arresting man, handsome and tall and muscular, and with a bearing that commanded attention in any gathering he was in. The servant equally acknowledged that part of why he saw Niu standing high above the rest was that Shun himself was smitten by the beautiful giant. But he had not been the only one to be so, and thus Shun thought his judgment was sound.

Niu, who had been the nanleshijia's baoan, or protector of the house, had been sold from the pleasure house precisely because of the effect he had on the jinan—the male prostitutes—in the house. The Cut Sleeve Nanleshijia was famous for being able to supply the most beautiful and nubile—and trained—virgins for the first bite of the peach for any man who could afford it. Niu, who was supposed to protect the virtue of the jinan in preparation, however, was prone to want to take this first bite himself. The premier virgin of the house, Xiu, was only barely saved from this fate on the night Niu had fled the service of the Duke of Shi, with the duke's warriors in hot pursuit.

Niu probably only made it out of Nantung with his skin because Shun, a servant of the house, had shown him a secret route—and had accompanied him and served his needs along the long road from Nantung to, first, Gusu, and then into the territory of Chu.

Shun, who pined for Niu, hadn't been allowed to serve all of Niu's needs, though. As the two folded into the lines of men following the army of Jili to join his service and seek their own fortunes and adventures, young, bright-eyed, and naïve young men increasingly became available. Of these, Niu had picked off the more handsome and innocent of the offerings and thus was quickly adding to his tally of bitten peaches—virgin males deflowered.

As they grew closer to the vanguard of the army, the crowds of men grew. Even in this throng, though, Niu stood out. Men naturally gravitated to him as a leader. And this night, when Niu and Shun had finally attained the central encampment of the King of Wu, down in the meadow, this phenomenon was repeated.

Niu hadn't asked for a retinue, and when the two, at Niu's instruction, had struck out up the hillside for a camping spot rather than down in the meadow, others had followed him. As Niu stood there enjoying the view of a thousand campfires flaring up in the darkening dusk and Shun finished laying out their blankets and started making a campfire, the men started to gather about them.

While Shun was setting the wood for the fire, he felt a tentative touch on his arm and looked up.

"May I help you with that?" The young soldier was shy and hesitant in his speech.

"I can manage," Shun said, returning the small smile the young man gave him.

"It would help for me to have something to do."

"You are afraid of the coming battles and wish something else to think of?" Shun asked. Then, when he saw that his thought had struck home and had caused embarrassment, he quickly added, "We are all afraid of that. Even the ones who boast of battle are afraid and are hiding their fright. Yes, of course, you may help. What is your name?"

"Rong."

"Where do you come from, Rong?" The two were working together, stacking the wood so that it would catch fire quicker but last longer. The young soldier was more adept at this than Shun was, which made Shun think he probably was used to these primitive conditions.

"I live three days' walk from Gusu," Rong answered. "My village is very small . . . and poor."

"And you've joined with the army to make your fortune?"

"More because there wasn't enough food for me to stay in the village. If I had not left, my parents would starve. There was not enough for three."

It had been said with sadness, but with acceptance. Looking closely at the young man, Shun could see that he wasn't asking for sympathy, only understanding of the condition that affected so many in the kingdom.

But Shun also saw that Rong was looking beyond him, at the figure of Niu, standing on the hillside, striking a majestic pose, and looking out over the encampment below. And what he saw in Rong's eyes was admiration—and longing—a longing not less than Shun himself had for Niu.

"You came up here to camp because of him, didn't you?"

"Yes. Isn't he magnificent? You are with him, aren't you? Do you serve him?"

"Not as I wish," Shun answered sadly. "But I can tell you that you need to be very careful with Niu." He took a long look at the youth. He was thin, but well muscled as any young man who engaged in hard work in a small village was. His face was strikingly handsome. Not quite as handsome as the young men of Nantung, of course, but their beauty was legendary. This young man had a gentleness about him and a smile that was engaging.

"Niu is a man's man, Rong. Do not look his way with longing if you do not know what that means."

"I . . . I don't understand," Rong said. And this told Shun what he suspected—and he felt an instant protectiveness for Rong.

"Niu lays with men, Rong. And he prefers men who have never lain with men before. And he is not constant; it is

53

all for just his enjoyment. Do you understand what I am saying, Rong?"

"Yes, I think so. You are with him? Did he lay with you too? And was he your first?"

"Yes to both," Shun said, remembering the harrowing trip up Langshan—Wolf Hill—in Nantung, where Niu was trying to get to a conquest who he had been pursuing for months before the monks of the Dragon Temple had ruined the young man. When he failed, he had taken out his anger and despair on Shun instead.

"But—"

Shun was unable to go on because Rong's attention now had refocused to farther down on the hillside, and when Shun looked there, his own line of thought was arrested.

Two soldiers, in the livery of the king's guard and mounted on war horses, were picking their way up the hillside to where the band of men had gathered around Niu to camp. They pulled up in front of Niu, said a few words to him, and then rode to the fringes of the camp and dismounted. The two unsaddled their horses and tied the reins off on trees at the fringe of the forest in a high stand of grass, where the horses could feed. They brought the saddles to near the fire and then sat at the fire and roasted a plucked and gutted fowl one of them had taken from a sack on his saddle. They spoke with the soldiers around them, but only sparingly.

Word made its way around the camp that they were pickets set out on the fringe of the greater encampment to warn of possible attack. The forces of the King of Chu were assumed to be not far away, and the Chu monarch was known for his dishonesty and cleverness. Battles were supposed to be conducted according to formal, long-held rules and on set battlefields. But the King of Chu didn't always remember this, according to the rumors.

Niu sat with the two imperial guards and chatted as wine was found and passed around. Shun melted into the shadows and watched, knowing what was likely to happen, but not having the power to do anything about it.

Rong was the one passing the wine. When he passed by Niu, who was leaning against the saddle of one of the guard's horses, Niu reach up and grabbed his arm and dragged Rong down beside him.

"Come rest a while, my fresh little peach," Niu declared with a jovial voice. "You have served the wine long enough. You are a perfect little peach. You are a peach, are you not?"

"Yes, sire, if you wish me to be," Rong answered in confusion, but he could not hide the admiration and looking in his eyes for Niu, who now was encircling him with one arm and patting him on the arms and breast with the other.

Shun's heart leapt in his chest. He wondered if Rong even knew that a peach was a ripe, untried young man. Rong, perhaps unknowingly, had just sealed his fate. Even without the wine he had drunk, Niu could not resist taking the first bite of a peach.

But, with the wine, Niu lost all inhibitions he might have had in the center of a group of skittish and randy soldiers, most of whom had not had a good fuck for days or weeks.

The young Rong didn't have a chance. When Niu, holding him close with one arm, moved a hand under his tunic and grabbed his thigh and then started working the hand up his leg, Rong strongly suspected what was happening. He could not have escaped then if he had wanted to. But he was conflicted, not knowing if he wanted to, smitten that Niu was showing him attention.

When Niu pulled his tunic over his head and ripped away his loin cloth, though, Rong knew for sure. Here his fear of the unknown and his anticipation swirled together, causing him to cry out in surprise and fear and to grunt and moan, as Niu's lips and teeth found his pert little nipples and Niu's hand grasped Rong's yang chu—his cock.

Shun looked on in horror and concern and disgust as the soldiers who were titillated by such taking—which was most of them—gathered around and egged Niu on with boisterous words and more than one hand getting such feel as they could on the young Rong's virginal body.

The imperial guard who had been sitting beside Niu cupped Rong's buttocks, remarking on how nicely rounded they were, rolled them apart, and began to finger Rong's tight

55

little hole, while another young soldier parted Niu's traveling tunic and took Niu's yang chu in his mouth.

To cheers from the gathered men, Niu, naked, his magnificent yang chu hard and curved upward for all to see, did pushups, his toes digging into the dirt of the hillside and the heel of his hands grinding into the grass on either side of Rong's shoulders, as Rong lay under him, his heaving belly on the inner curve of the saddle and his rounded little butt cheeks pointed to the heavens and split in two by Niu's pumping yang chu. Rong was grasping Niu's wrists in a white-knuckled ineffectiveness and initially writhed under Niu and cried out for mercy, a mercy that did not come.

One of the imperial guardsmen quieted Rong by kneeling under Rong's bobbing head, taking his own hard yang chu in his hand, and giving Rong's face something to bob on. And Niu's stamina in the fuck eventually made Rong's body go limp and completely accepting.

The gathered men had cast bets upon which stroke Niu would give up his seed inside the bitten peach, with Niu winning if none guessed correctly. Such was Niu's skill and stamina in the stroking that they all lost, their higher number having been reached well before Niu was finished. Thus Niu became a much richer man that night.

So impressive was his performance that, when he had finished biting the peach and had drunk another flagon of wine, he accepted the begging of other men to go with him and mined many another hole that night. But before Niu would pick his next conquest, his deep voice could be heard ringing out. "Who here, who else here is a peach? Who wants me to pop his pit?"

Hearing the erstwhile friends of a young lad answering that call on the young man's behalf, Niu took another swig of the wine and lurched off toward his new conquest.

Rong was pulled up from the saddle by four men, each to a limb, and was carried off to the forest and shared out by the four.

It was here, hours later, that, having waited for the camp to quiet down for the night, Shun sought and found

Rong, lying on his back in a fern bed, whimpering and moaning quietly.

Shun had brought salves with him and knelt beside Rong's body and began to rub the salve on the youth's bruised flesh.

"Have you come to have me too?" Rong murmured. He opened his legs and raised them up, heels dug in the damp earth, resigned to the next in a succession of men in the night.

"No, Rong. I do not take other men. I'm sorry. I tried to warn you about Niu. You could have hidden rather than serving the wine."

"Do you think he will have me again?" Rong asked.

Shun looked down into the youth's face. He saw that he was still smitten with Niu—if anything, more smitten now, having been possessed by the magnificent yang chu of Niu's. He started to say something, but then he locked his jaw. Who was he to say anything? Didn't he beg for Niu to take him again?

"I don't think so, Rong. Not unless you had a palace to give him. His ardor is for biting the peach."

"But he could, couldn't he? He could lay with me again? He lays with you, doesn't he?"

"That's what I tried to tell you before, Rong—before the imperial guards arrived. No, he has not lain with me again—not after that first time. He hardly knows I am here. Perhaps if you were a king and could offer him a palace. Or if your name was Xiu. I have only seen him look on one person with love that is more than a carnal desire to be first. Xiu is a jinan in preparation in the Nantung . . ."

But Shun looked down at Rong and saw that he needed no explanation. The young soldier, more worldly wise now than when the sun rose that morning, was already mercifully fast asleep. Shun lay down beside the young soldier and hugged him tight to keep him warm through the reminder of the night.

* * * *

Shun was awake at dawn, finding himself alone in the fern bed. He rose and walked out of the forest and into a camp

57

of muttering, hung-over soldiers stumbling here and there and making ready to be on the move again. Rong was there too, moving around with his head cast down, not speaking to anyone, but being very industrious.

Shun wondered what he should say to Rong about the previous night, but when the young soldier looked up, his face pointed to Shun, Shun could see that Rong wanted to act like the previous night hadn't happened at all—that Rong wanted to act as if he didn't even recognize who Shun was.

Perhaps that's for the best, Shun thought, and he went off to find Niu.

But he didn't find Niu, and when he asked if anyone knew where he was, he was told that Niu had left before dawn with the two imperial guards. Gathering up Niu's and his possessions and strapping the bundle to his back, Shun gave a little sigh and started to work his way down the hillside, bound for the encampment in the meadow. At least Niu is so tall, he thought, that he will be easy to pick out among the crowds down here.

At that moment, Niu was down in a tent in the meadow, nearly in the center of encampment, where the tents were larger and of the best quality.

He had been bathed and given a new, silk hanfu—robe—and was standing nearly at attention between the two imperial guards he had met on the hillside the previous day. In the morning Niu had found out that the guards weren't on the hillside to be sentries; they had been sent there especially to seek Niu out in the interest of someone much higher in the rankings of the army.

"Come closer," said a refined voice from across the room.

Pressed by the guards, Niu took three steps closer to the canopied bed with the damask drapes. A bejeweled hand reached out beyond the foot of the canopied bed.

"Take your robe off."

With the help of the two guards, Niu drew his hanfu over his head. He was standing there in all of his magnificence.

"Yes, he is pleasing. You have scavenged well. You may go now." The bejeweled hand beckoned the guards away. "Come. Come into the bed."

Niu climbed into the bed on his knees, finding himself kneeling between the spread legs of the King of Wu, who had untied his sash and spread his hanfu off of his naked body.

At a signal from the king, attendants closed the damask drapes around the bed as Niu moved closer in to the king's body and the king lifted his ankles to Niu's shoulders.

For the next hour all that those inside the tent but outside the enclosed bed could hear were the cries and moans of the king and the grunts of Niu, although no one was there to tell them they could not enjoy watching the wave-like motion of the red lacquered bed with its fine silk drapes swaying.

The king lay on his back on his pillows, his hands tied to the headboard over his head with red silk roping, crying out, "Yes, yes, punish me," as Niu knelt between his spread thighs and rhythmically pumped his cock in and out of the royal hole. Niu had a multithong leather whip with knotted ends in his hand and was switching it on the king's heaving chest, listening for where the king was showing he had reached the thin edge between his pain and his pleasure. The king was in ecstasy.

Far away from the tent Shun was hunting for Niu so diligently that he belatedly heard the frightened cries rising above the usual hubbub of a military camp coming awake and packing up for a march. He thus wasn't aware of the horsemen of the raiding party from the army of the Chu until they were upon him.

He was of no concern to them; they were making a wild dash for the center of the encampment, for the imperial tents. But Shun stumbled in the way of one of the horsemen who, in irritation, raised his sword and brought it down on Shun's back. Shun went down in a heap. Behind the horsemen, in a wedge, were foot soldiers of the Chu army moving resolutely through the parting panicked crowd before them.

A fiercely angry Niu, naked except for the sword in his hand, swept the damask drapes of the imperial bed open just as the first horsemen ripped the side of the tent with his sword and rode into the center of the space within. Niu stood protectively over the vulnerable and prone body of the king, slow to react only because he was so besotted with sword work of an entirely different variety.

Niu and the horseman exchanged parries of their swords as another horseman was working his way into the tent. The King of Wu's men had recovered from the shock of the attack, though, and were also rushing under the canvas, swords raised.

Having run the first horseman through with the king's sword and turning toward the second one, Niu stood his ground over the torso of the king.

* * * *

Months later, as the forces of Wu and Chu feinted and parried in skirmishes back and forth across the border separating their territories, The attention of Wu was turned toward one of its border prefectures. The anger and determination of Jili, King of Wu, was almost palpable as he unleashed his cavalry, war chariots, and bronze and iron weapons—all battlefield levelers that his enemies had never before encountered—on the rebel town of Anyi, which had switched allegiance to the kingdom of Chu. Within hours of receiving the message that the Lord of Anyi would not send tribute and yield in the season of homage, Jili and his loyal servant and trusted chamberlain, Niu, obedient servant to the king everywhere but in the confines of the royal bed, riding three strides to his rear, galloped out of his encampment on the opposite banks of the river Xi, which separated Wu from Chu. Jili's forces had already been inside Chu territory when Anyi, at his army's rear, across the river, had defected. That the forces of Anyi put up a stout defense at the imperial army's recrossing of the Xi only added to Jili's indignation and anger.

The Lord of Anyi, Zhu Xin Yi by personal name, would need to be taught a lesson that none of the other vassals to Jili's building empire would forget for the ages.

Once across the Xi, and sweeping the army of Anyi aside like a misting of spring insects, the forces of Jili descended on the city of Anyi, attacking from four directions, the foot infantry from the southwest, double-horsed chariots from the northwest and southeast, and Jili at the head of his vaunted cavalry from the northeast, where the Lord of Anyi had planned a retreat, if that proved necessary, into the surrounding hills.

Jili wanted to seize the seasoned men of the ruling family of the Lord of Anyi alive and thus had taken command of the rising hills that his spies within Anyi had told him the family of the Lord of Anyi would attempt to flee into if the battle went against them.

The King of Wu had put out the order that Anyi was to be leveled and every tenth man, woman, and child within it put to the sword as a warning to any others thinking of holding out on Jili's drive to unify the Chinese empire. But he had given strict orders that Zhu Xin Yi and any sons not killed in battle were to be captured alive and delivered to him at the temple of the tiger atop Taiyuan Shan, the Lord of Anyi's sacred spot.

And so it was.

By design, Jili had ridden out to the temple with the royal hostages of all his vassal states that were being held to ensure the loyalty of every other vassal lord. He wanted them to see what happened to those who rebelled. As Jili, the King of Wu, cruelly spurred his battle stallion, panting and foaming at the mouth from five hours of fast gallop and three hours of close-in combat, up the slope toward the Taiyuan Shan temple, he turned and scowled at Niu, who had fallen to five strides behind him instead of the required three.

"Keep up, servant—or . . ."

Niu was panting and ragged of breath as they reached the summit. He had fought hard—harder than Jili, because it had been Niu at every close engagement with the enemy who had shielded Jili from all sides, making the aging king look like an invincible warrior. As tired as Niu was, he was only the required three strides behind his master—close enough to throw himself from his steed at the moment of realization that Jili wanted to dismount, so he could fling his body, prostate, in the mud at the side of Jili's stallion, in time to provide a stepping stone for his master's dismount.

Jili trampled heavily and with muddied hide-covered boots on his chamberlain's back as he dismounted and strode into the temple, with Niu scrambling to take up the required three paces in his wake, followed closely behind by the quivering hostages from the other lands where Jili held sway.

At Niu's side was the young prince, Jiayi, Jili's third son, who the King of Wu had brought on campaign to start toughening up the young man, barely in his majority. Jili hadn't brought his first two sons, because they could not be put in jeopardy while the king was on the battlefield. As the third son, Jiayi barely mattered. That didn't keep the young man from carefully assessing everything he saw for opportunity. What he often was assessing since coming on campaign, though, was the muscular and arousing body of the chamberlain, Niu. Jiayi had never lain with a man before—which rumor had it would be enticing to Niu—although it was more because Jiayi wanted a worthy sexual master than that he had an aversion to having a male lover. He could not help but wonder about Niu, so subservient to the king in public but yet rumored to be the king's master in private. Sometime on this campaign Jiayi was determined to test out the legends of Niu's yang chu—and of his desires to conquer virgin channels.

The cavalry outriders who had captured and brought Zhu Xin Yi and his four surviving sons to the temple stood guard around the five cowering prisoners. They had been beaten, but, with the exception of Zhu Xin Yi himself, who was bleeding profusely and whose right arm had been almost severed in battle, four of the five men of the House of Anyi were alive enough. Zhu Xin Yi stood, bent painfully but defiant, alongside his only slightly wounded eldest son, who glowered at Jili menacingly as the conqueror strode into the temple's central chamber. The room they occupied was a stone, vaulted-ceiling space adorned only by a vermillion-painted altar standing in the very center under an open sky light, which cast the rays of the noonday sun directly down on the House of Anyi's ceremonial sacred heart, it's ancestral altar. Off to the sides were alcoves draped with cloth, where the priests of the temple were said to deflower their initiates.

This was why the Jili had chosen this temple for this ceremony—from a perverse amusement of the knowledge of how the priests here recruited into their ranks.

Zhu Xin Yi's youngest surviving son, merely a boy, whimpered slightly, no doubt at the sounds of carnage and sight of the rising smoke from the doomed capital city of Anyi below the mountain slope, but his sobs subsided at a sharp look from his father's eyes. The two middle sons clung to each other as they huddled on the floor, but the difference between them was noticeable. One, the second son, a sword gash laying open a wound on his forehead, had his eyes closed and his face buried into the bosom of the third son, who, blood-covered but largely unmarked himself, looked out at the approaching Jili more in curiosity than anything else.

"Has the Lord of Anyi agreed to yield?" Jili bellowed. Everyone in the confines of the temple shuddered noticeably at the master's declaration, even Zhu Xin Yi. Although advanced in age, Jili was a magnificent figure, perfectly formed, heavily muscled, astonishingly handsome, and carrying himself with grace and supreme confidence as the unifier of kingdoms that he was becoming through his own determination and talent— and on the strength of his modern weaponry.

"Majesty . . ." the captain of the cavalry began in a voice edged with fear and dread. He could neither lie nor tell the truth. Zhu Xin Yi had turned to stone in his recalcitrance. The cavalry officer knew that anything he said at this point was sure to bring down the wrath of his master.

Jili saved him the indignity. The cavalry captain was a good soldier. Jili could not spare him.

"No matter," he said with a sneer. "Once disloyal is one time too many and it cannot be mended. The Lord of Anyi is no more. I must have a new lord. One of the sons must do. But which one? And all must know of my suzerainty over him." At the mouthing of the word "all," Jili let his gaze cover all of those gathered, ensuring that the "representatives" of the other vassal lords were fully aware of the gravity and symbolism of what was about to happen.

Jili snapped his fingers, and his faithful drudge in public, Niu, bent almost double and eyes firmly planted on the ground, stepped up into Jili's peripheral vision. "Yes, master?"

"You know what I require."

"Yes, master," Niu responded. "Not the eldest; he is as unmalleable as the father. He would rebel again as soon as we recrossed the Xi to pursue the King of Chu to his lair in Danyang. And not the youngest; he belongs with the women." At this, a gasp escaped the gathering of hostages standing at the edge of the temple behind Jili. All knew that the women of the House of Anyi had already gone to join his ancestors.

"Of the two remaining," Niu continued in a hesitant voice, "one will die anyway of that festering wound. The remaining one looks out at the world with curiosity, even in the present circumstances. He may be trainable."

"Ah, you have chosen wisely, I think, chamberlain. So it will be."

The third son, Jiayi thought, his mind soaring to the possibility that Niu was sending a message to him by picking the third son. And was this perhaps an omen of the future beyond the present circumstance? There were those at the court in Gusu, egged on by his own mother, who suggested Jiayi should be Jili's successor—and perhaps sooner rather than later.

While speaking, Jili unbuckled his belt and let it and his sword fall—into the hands of Niu, who dove for it, lest it hit the ground, although he had to sink to his knees to prevent it from doing so.

Carrying the sword while genuflecting, Niu backed away from the altar area. Guided by Jiayi's own helpful hand, he backed all the way into one of the alcoves, and Jiayi partially pulled the drapes to the opening together, so that the two of them were alone in the alcove but could still watch the proceedings through the slight opening in the drapes.

"Captain, the handsome one," the king commanded, clapping his hands. "The one with the curious eye. The ceremony of reclaimed suzerainty of the fallen enemy. Now!"

The captain motioned to the two heftiest of his men guarding the captives, who pulled the third son up and away from his mortally wounded brother. As they stripped the struggling captive, the remaining guards manhandled the father and eldest son into submission, holding them firmly, facing the altar.

At the captain's command, the two cavalrymen, one at each arm of the third son of the Lord of Anyi, pulled his naked body around to the side of the altar facing Jili and held him down, facing away from Jili, belly flat on the altar and face turned to his still-struggling and cursing elder brother and father.

In the alcove, Jiayi placed a hand on Niu's arm. He could feel that the man was trembling slightly. "You know what is about transpire, do you not?" Jiayi whispered to Niu.

"Yes, of course," was the stiff answer. Niu had been reserved with Jiayi ever since he had come into service with the king. He didn't fool Jiayi, though. He was sure that the reserve was because Niu wanted him.

"I have heard that the third son of the House of Anyi is a peach. Do you believe that is possible? He is so handsome and well formed, and certainly could have lain with a man if he had wanted to. Kings and princes do as they like. So, our king is about to bite into a very ripe peach. How do you feel about that?"

Jiayi smiled at the low growl he heard rising from deep inside Niu. He moved to in front of Niu, who towered over him, then he raised his robes from behind, took Niu's hands into his and laid them on the nakedness of his waist under the robes.

"I am a peach too, Niu. Ripe for the bite. And willing. In fact, as a prince of Wu, I command it."

Jiayi laughed a deep, throaty laugh, as he felt Niu's hands on his waist tremble—but, significantly, not withdraw at Jiayi's bold offer. One of Niu's hands went around Jiayi's waist and palmed the nakedness of his flat belly between robe and flesh. Jiayi felt Niu fumbling with the sash on his battle robe with the other hand, and then move his fingers between Jiayi's plump orbs. The eyes of both of them were still focused on what was happening on the altar. Jiayi sighed and leaned back into Niu's body, enjoying the tightening of his father's

Chamberlain's palm on his belly and the invasion of the fingers.

At the altar Jili was also letting his battle robe fall open to reveal his magnificent body and a long, thick, and hardened phallus. As he approached the hind quarters of the young prince of Anyi, two other cavalrymen sprang forth to spread the young man's legs and to pull his buttocks cheeks away to reveal a pulsating rosebud of an anus.

Other servants came forward to anoint Jili's yang chu with perfumed oil.

With a cry of triumph and uttering the sacred creeds of the House of Wu, Jili then strode up to and between the Anyi prince's spread legs, positioned his bulging cock cap at the young man's hole with a steady hand, and then thrust hard and deep inside him.

The young prince of Anyi cried out in pain and violation and writhed, chest heaving and panting, face contorted in the taking, while Jili thrust in deep, searching motions inside him, seeking the resting of his heavy, quivering balls on top of his younger conquest's. And then thrusting, again and again.

Such was the attention riveted on the action at the altar that no one heard Jiayi's little cry of triumph as Niu thrust an even longer and thicker phallus than the king's up into the prince's channel from the rear. Jiayi arched his back to Niu and his knees got weak. But Niu held him fast with the big hand palming the young man's belly.

As Jili stroked, symbolically forging his renewed mastery over the House of Anyi as well as enjoying himself immensely, the young prince slowly fell under the master taker's spell as well—so that before long, not long before he gave up his own seed against the vermillion flanks of the sacred House of Anyi family altar, the young prince was crying out for more and moving with the taking rather than against it.

If he was doing so more out of a survival instinct and cleverness than real enjoyment, he revealed none of this to his king.

Meanwhile Jiayi, the prince of Wu, gasped and sighed as his father's chamberlain spurted his seed once, twice, and then a third time deep inside Jiayi's belly.

"Again, again," the young prince murmured. But Niu was already extracting his yang chu and adjusting his robe. He turned the young prince to the side in the alcove, let him sink to the floor in a long moan, and then strode out to be near the altar when his king needed him. He was smiling to himself. It had been days since he'd been able to leave the king's side long enough to bite into a peach—and this one was a luscious one. A channel so tight and a peach so ready and willing that Niu had given up his seed almost immediately.

The highly vocal capitulation of the Anyi prince on the altar infuriated and demoralized the elder men of the House of Anyi more than if the young man had been ritually cut up into quarters on the altar. They knew the rituals of the House of Wu. They knew that the new Lord of Anyi had now been chosen and, having been brought under the control of Jili in both body and soul, would be trained to rule a rebuilt Anyi to his master's dictates. And, to the shame of the House of Anyi, they now could see that he would do so willingly and as the catamite of the evil emperor-to-be.

It was almost in relief and preference that, after Jili had spilled his possessing seed deep inside the new lord of Anyi, Zhu Xin Yi and his remaining sons were led out, through the ranks of the pale and sweating hostages, onto the steps of the temple, overlooking the dying city below them, to meet their public appointment with the avenging sword.

As they had been led out, the captain of the guard approached the King of Wu and whispered, "The youngest son, sire. He is very nubile. Perhaps as a reward to your bodyguards . . . before he is dispatched . . . or perhaps in the dispatching . . ."

"No, enough," the king declared with a wave of his hand. "Let him perish in dignity with the rest."

If it was a slight that, after Niu had prostrated himself beside Jili's waiting stallion again when the victory party descended the temple stairs, the new Lord of Anyi, sore but sporting a lopsided grin, was placed on a horse only one stride behind the master and two in front of Niu, the chamberlain made no sign of feeling it so.

Now Niu had a delicious secret of his own. While Jili was doing his duty to consolidate his power, Niu had been debauching his son.

Later that night, in the tent of the King of Wu on the banks of the River Xi, Niu stood in the shadows and in attendance to satisfy Jili's every whim as the new Lord of Anyi, in diaphanous leggings and burnished bared torso, danced to the tune of the lutes and thin, pitch-perfect voices of the singsong girls. The young man was well made. Lithe but well muscled. He obviously was clever and good with sword play, having survived the battle unscathed, and he evidenced this with the sensuousness of his movement to the music.

The prince Jiayi came up behind Niu, placed a hand on his buttocks, and raised his lips to first kiss Niu on the ear and then to whisper how he wanted Niu to visit his tent that night—that he wanted more of Niu's yang chu.

Niu turned his head and gave Jiayi an even stare and said, "I will be busy tonight. I have taken from you what I want. Perhaps if you were a king . . ."

Giving Niu a thunderous look, Jiayi turned and flounced out of the tent.

Niu turned his attention back to the light from the fire to watch as the heir to the House of Anyi danced closer and closer to Jili, who was propped up on pillows in the light of the lamps at the four corners of the central area of the tent marked by the maroon carpet intricately woven in the golds and blues of the House of Wu. Jili was draped in a robe of gold thread, but he was reclining on the pillows and his robe had fallen open, revealing a sword of prodigious length and width curving up from his belly and bobbing with the rhythm of the young man's dance. There was no doubt that he found his young captive enticing.

And for his part, the new Lord of Anyi was entranced. He had been taken with the master sword once, his first sheathing, and he could not take his eyes off it as he danced. Being clever enough to survive to this point, he wanted to convey that he could not wait to be pierced with it again and again.

The young man was on his knees on the lush carpet now, between Jili's spread legs, his torso undulating, but dipping ever lower. Until at last his lips were at the bobbing bulb of Jili's manhood—and opening over the bulb, and taking it inside his mouth, and sucking it close.

Jili looked up into the shadows at where he knew Niu stood in ever-ready service. He snapped his fingers and said, "Only you other than the new Lord of Anyi."

"Yes, master," Niu responded, then. Then Niu turned in either direction, motioning the vigilant, yet studiously blind guards and the singsong girls out of the tent. They immediately left in graceful silence.

Niu remained, watching, as the young prince heated up the master, making him moan and sigh at the young captive's attentions in a way that none but Niu was permitted to observe or hear. No hint of weakness would be permitted.

At length, Jili pulled the young lord's face from his cock and reached down at his belly and ripped away the diaphanous material. He then lifted the young man and set him firmly and cruelly down on his club of a yang chu. The young lord cried out in pain as he had done before, only once before having been taken and not prepared in any way. But writhe as he unwillingly did—as he clearly wanted to be taken again—he was able to give no resistance to Jili. The King of Wu merely raised him and lowered him ever farther down the blade of the piercing sword with strong hands gripping his waist.

Jili fucked on forever—long after the young lord had spouted his own seed up Jili's hard, muscled belly.

Nearly exhausted, the young lord whimpered in thanksgiving when Jili finally lifted him off his bludgeon and let him fall over to the side. The young man started to slither away, across the rug, but he should have known that Jili was only toying with him; the master's cock was as hard and thick and long as it ever had been.

The young lord squeaked in shock and fear and trembling, as Jili came up on his knees and grabbed the young man around the waist again and held him there, belly to carpet, as Jili encased the young lord's thighs between his knees and thrust down inside him again and rode him and rode him and rode him.

Niu heard a sound at the back entrance to the tent and turned to see that prince Jiayi was spying on what was transpiring in the center of the tent. But when Jiayi saw that Niu had found him out, a hateful look spread across his face and he withdrew.

The new Lord of Anyi was completely conquered and nearly comatose when Jili at last cried out in his own ejaculation and was finished with him. The ruler snapped his fingers, and Niu lifted the nearly unconscious and whimpering young man in his arms and carried him to the front entrance of the tent. He muttered instructions to the guards outside, who carried the young man away, and then drew back inside the tent and pulled down and firmly tied off the flap covering the entrance.

Niu turned and moved toward the center of the tent. As he did so, he was untying the knot of his own robe. He let the robe fall open and fall away at his sides, revealing his own well-muscled, sinewy torso and a proud yang chu rising hard out from his center.

Jili was on his knees at the center of the carpet, facing Niu.

"Are you pleased? Did I do well, master?" Jili murmured.

"Well enough, but I think you have been enjoying the new Lord of Anyi too well. I think you need to be punished," Niu was standing taller now, his voice hard, more demanding. The chamberlain was now in his element. He had taught Jili well, but it was now time to remind him who the real master was in private.

"Yes, yes, master. I need to be punished," Jili whimpered. He slithered across the carpet on his knees to where Niu was standing and took his chamberlain's cock in both hands and fed it into his mouth. Niu stood there, pelvis hunched forward, and pulled Jili's hair and slapped his face with open palms while the servant king pumped his cock in and out his mouth.

"The pallet. Now!" Niu commanded.

"Yes, master," Jili answered in a whispered tone after taking his mouth off Niu's cock. He stumbled back to the side of the tent, in the shadows, where animal skins, layered thick on a low platform, lay between four sturdy lacquered-wood posts. Niu tied the old ruler's wrists off on the two posts at the head of the bed and lifted and spread his legs and tied them off high on the posts at the foot of the bed, forcing pillows under the small of his back to raise the King's buttocks to the level of Niu's pelvis.

Then, while alternating fucking Jili's hole hard and roughly and slapping his buttocks red with hand and riding crop, Niu showed he was the real master of the House of Wu as the king moaned and groaned and asked for more and spilled his seed on the banks of the Xi River over and over again in the ecstasy of the mastering.

In the ensuing days, Niu spurned the advances of Prince Jiayi more than once, telling him that since he no longer was a virgin, he was of no interest to Niu.

One evening as Niu was taking a stroll before returning to the king's tent to apply the discipline the king thrived on, Jiayi approached him and, with a smirk, said, "You have said that a king is as arousing to you as a virgin, have you not?"

"Yes, I did say that," Niu said, his face showing the confusion that was on his mind.

"Then perhaps I will see you in my tent before dawn," the young prince said. Then he laughed, turned, and strode away.

Niu could not decipher what Jiayi meant, but a feeling of dread overcame him and he rushed back to the king's tent in a stumbling run.

The drapes were drawn around the pallet of the king. Niu approached and with trembling hands pulled the drapes aside. King Jili was lying on his back, naked. The handle of a knife protruded from his lower chest and he was looking at Niu with unseeing eyes.

Niu immediately knew what had happened, who was responsible for this. He did not have the least doubt that even now the princes of Wu number one and two were lying in similar death stances back in the capital of Gusu.

What Niu didn't know was whether Jiayi's invitation to him just now was to a tryst with the new king or to a trap. Niu would be the natural suspect for this dastardly act of regicide.

The one thing that Niu knew for sure, though, was that he could not test out which of these alternatives was true. He knew that when the king's body was found, he, Niu, would need to be as far away from the encampment on the banks of the River Xi as possible.

Chapter Six: Bitter Fruit for Ping

Deng Qiao, owner of all of the cotton mills within sight of Langshan—Wolf Hill—at the fringe of the Yangtze riverside town of Nantung, sighed as he wiggled his hips into the pillows and held his young consort's silken black-haired head in his lap. Ping, the singer musician, who Qiao had bought from the Cut Sleeve Nanleshijia—men's pleasure house—was working vigorously on trying to bring Qiao's cock alive, but it was slow going.

Ping lifted his head and looked up into Qiao's eyes. Seeing concern there, he asked, "Why so sad, sire? Am I not pleasing you?"

"You always please me, little songbird," Qiao replied. "It is only a small spasm. It will pass. Please continue. Your lovely mouth is taking my mind off the world."

What Qiao didn't say was that it was more than a small spasm he was feeling in his chest. He was feeling a hint of the inevitable. And above that, he was thinking of Ming Lei, the accursed pirate, who had begun to worry the shipping off the mouth of the Yangtze River. He had lost two cotton goods shipments in the last full phase of the moon, and his fortune was beginning to sift through his fingers.

Qiao cursed his luck. Forty years building his fortune and begetting sons off of the ugly but fruitful and wealthy Meilin, and now, when he had entered the reward-enjoyment phase of his life, the double curse. He had nurtured the young and handsome Ping, knowing full well that someday he could leave his family behind at the court of the King of Wu in Gusu and retreat to his Nantung home with a little songbird like Ping, to enjoy his mature years fucking how and who he pleased. And it wasn't just that. He truly loved Ping; he had desired him for years before he could touch him, acting as the patron for the young man's training at the nanleshijia, all for the privilege of taking that first bite of the peach and then savoring it for years afterward. And then, when Ping had matured enough, Qiao had extended the invitation of sharing the Tea of the Full Moon with him, afraid, even though he was the patron summoning a jinan—a male prostitute—he had paid for, that there would be a form of rejection. He was confident that Ping would accept the offer—that was his responsibility to his nanleshijia master—but Qiao loved Ping and wanted it to be a union of mutual acceptance and desire.

Ping had been as shy as a bride. Handsome and beautifully formed, Ping had been demur and had trembled even before the touch. He had sat there, on the nanleshijia pavilion platform, under the moon as it opened wide into full blossom—just as Qiao envisioned Ping opening wide to him, and tasted of the tea Qiao had offered, the specially imbued tea that heightened some senses and dulled others, hardened the yang chu, the cock—and loosened inhibitions and opened the channel.

Ping was already sighing softly as Qiao moved his hand within the folds of Ping's hanfu. The youth flinched as Qiao took a nipple between his thumb and forefinger and rolled it—but Ping did none of the things that signaled rejection or reluctance. Instead, he moaned in a sound that came up from the very depths of him. Throwing all caution and ceremony aside, Qiao clawed at the sash of both his and Ping's hanfu, and he was pulling the loved one he had waited for—not

74

patiently—but waited for, for years, into his lap and was assaulting Ping's virginal hole with his ready cock, barely giving the younger man sufficient time to open to him. Ping lost his *chenchieh*, his chastity, quickly in a violent, passionate taking. But, though he cried out upon full possession and panted heavily and whimpered at the taking, Ping gave himself fully, giving Qiao no cause to lessen his love or his insatiable desire for his handsome vassal. And thus was how Ping rose many levels of importance in the House of the Cut Sleeve.

Although it was customary for patrons to visit their *jinan* at the house of pleasure and even for the *jinan* to entertain men other than their patron, Ping had been separated from the opportunities of the *nanleshijia* and become Qiao's Nantung retreat consort in exchange for comfort and a position in the household and a promise of a large inheritance. But now, a few short months later, Qiao was having trouble performing as he desired.

The second curse was connected with the first. Qiao was dying. Knowing that something was wrong inside, he had accepted the diagnosis—even had resigned himself to it beforehand. But he was keeping it to himself. In his world any sign of weakness could be a death sentence, a massive shock to the balances within a large household. His golden years would not be gold; they would not even be silver. They would be bitter, and they would not even be years. Bitter fruit. Bitter fruit indeed. He sighed again, willing his cock to harden, wanting to forget the real and the ironic in fucking the handsome Ping.

Part of the problem, Qiao reasoned as he flinched and felt a little spark of arousal when Ping took his balls in his mouth and started rolling them around in his cheeks while working on Qiao's cock with his long, slender fingers, was that he had felt little warmth in Ping recently. There had been plenty of fire in Ping's belly back in the pleasure house, when their trysts were a ritualized game. But here, in his own house, months after the biting of the peach, with no mystery or anticipation—or perhaps, Qiao had to admit, not having the variety of a young, virile yang chu in addition to Qiao's withered one, Ping's desires had gone dull. It was nothing in what Ping willingly exhibited; it was in what he could not hide.

There was progress on the rising of Qiao's cock, but at a glacial pace. Seeing the problem and not wanting to have to stand by in service and watch this upstart Ping worming his way into Qiao's heart for hours on end yet, Qiao's chamberlain leaned down and whispered in his master's ear.

"Perhaps some entertainment, master. I have something that you may find very helpful. A dancer, all the way from the land down under. Young, strong, old enough, but not appearing so. Perhaps if the master pleases, and Ping is unable . . ."

Ping snapped his head up, instantaneously sensing the danger to his position. He tried, not altogether successfully, not to flash a hateful look at the chamberlain. It was always household struggles for power in the homes of the Wu kingdom elite. Ping threatened the chamberlain's position, who, in turn, held Ping in check. But the balance had changed. Ping was on the ascent—unless the chamberlain could somehow neutralize that. The dancer hadn't just been passing through nor had he been an afterthought of any sort. The dark little down-under dancer was a card the chamberlain was playing.

Sensing the competition and knowing that Qiao was aroused by music, which is why he had been attracted to the singer musician Ping, the jinan put a little more effort into arousing Qiao's manhood, using his tongue more on the slit in the cock bulb and swallowing Qiao whole and putting pressure on the root with his teeth. Qiao squirmed and gave a little moan and thickened—a bit, not much.

"Shih, shih. Yes, yes," Qiao answered in slight irritation. "If I am paying for a dancing boy, let me see the dancing boy." He was waving dismissively at the chamberlain. But the chamberlain knew his master well from long service. He had acquired an edge.

"Not a dancing boy," the chamberlain said as he leaned down and murmured to Qiao and said in a silky, suggestive voice. "Fully manned—with a man's talents and full experience—but the aspect and size of a boy—although, as you will see, not everywhere. Like Yongrui. You remember Yongrui?"

The chamberlain looked down at his reclining master with the countenance of pure innocence. Ping gazed sideways at the chamberlain in suspicion as he worked Qiao's cock in his mouth.

Yes, Qiao definitely did remember Yongrui. A beautiful boy—but not really a boy. And not even a youth. He had the gift of perpetual youth. He had been Qiao's tutor, his laoshi, and, in addition to teaching young Qiao the classics, he had also taught him the ways of the world—which included teaching him how to take a cock—Yongrui's—and then when Qiao himself was fully manned, Yongrui had given himself to his student, fully, and thus taught him the pleasure that Qiao had craved all of his adult life, while he was doing his duty to his ancestors, and that he now was trying to fully enjoy on Langshan mountain.

Ping felt the stirring of the cock in his mouth and the rumble of a sigh stirring through the master's body. Who was this Yongrui, he wondered. And in what way could he endanger Ping's position? How was he to know that Yongrui had died when Ping was still a boy—in fact just before Qiao had turned his eyes to the promising young, beautiful boy whose training had just started in the Cut Sleeve Nanleshijia? Still, Ping sensed a present danger. The chamberlain should not be this pleased.

Music started from singsong girls beyond the Western Pavilion curtains, and a young boy minced onto the tatami matting in front of the bed of pillows where Qiao was reclined and Ping was bent over his half-hard cock.

But it wasn't a boy. Qiao could see that now. It was a young man. The chamberlain had called him the dark beauty from down under. He was small, but perfectly formed, with the cock and balls of a man much larger than he was evident inside the diaphanous transparent, billowy pantaloons that were his only clothing other than the gold-bangled belt that was duplicated in bands around his ankles, wrists, and biceps. The richly dark-skinned dancer moved with supreme, undulating grace. He never was still the entire time he danced. And he danced beautifully, mesmerizingly.

Qiao was interested, but only slightly aroused—at least by the dance of the dark beauty.

When Ping looked up, however, he was smitten and drowned in the beauty of the movement of the dancer—and not just by his movement. As small as he was everywhere else, he had a yang chu to rival any man's. The discrepancy in sizes was enough to send Ping's arousal soaring. And this was transferred in the love he made to Qiao's cock. The electricity of Ping's arousal flowed through to Qiao, and his cock became almost as proudly erect as it had when he had first taken Ping.

Seeing his chance and his need to solidify his position, Ping rose, took Qiao's cock in his hand, and slowly descended his ass canal on the now-hard member. He did so, though, with his back against Qiao's chest. Ping sensed—correctly—that the dancer was the catalyst. That his own arousal for the dancer had flowed through to Qiao. And he knew without a doubt that it was Qiao's arousal that had to be maintained. Qiao encircled Ping's chest with his arms as Ping fucked himself on Qiao's cock and tweaked his young consort's nipples. Ping answered in the moanings that he knew were expected and desired—and that were further arousing to the master. He turned his head and they kissed.

When Ping turned his attention back to the dancer, he gasped and gulped in breath. The dancer had shed his pantaloons. He was holding his overlong cock in his hand and swinging it as he undulated his body. And there was a thick golden bar piercing the head of his cock.

Ping had never seen such as this before—and it put him into an arousal such as he had never felt before. His channel and hips went into overdrive, and his groans and moans mounted to meet the cries of desire coming from Qiao. Qiao exploded in a flowing that he had not managed in nearly a month.

Yes, he could die happy, he thought. If he could just experience this once again each day before he died. Memories of Yongrui swam up and clutched at him, and his love for his Ping overflowed in tears of appreciation.

Ping sighed and snuggled back into the embrace of his master, feeling the vitality of the old man wash away, knowing that his position in the house of Deng Qiao had been safe gained for at least one more day.

The chamberlain ushered the dancer out of the room. He was not really displeased at Ping's success with Qiao. In fact, he was very pleased with Ping's reaction to the dark beauty from down under. It fit into his plans precisely.

Later that night, Qiao stirred in his sleep—the pain in his chest almost unbearable. He could not sleep because of it. Would this be the night, he wondered. He had been told it would not be this soon—but soon enough. But how does mere man know of the plans of the ancestors anyway? Qiao thought bitterly—but not without acceptance of inevitability, which was blessed by a sense of peace.

He turned and reached for Ping. But he was not there.

He rose, worried about where Ping had gone. Wanting him there, holding him, if this was to be the night. On silent feet and covered only by a soft, cotton robe, Qiao padded to the chamber that was Ping's when Qiao preferred solitude.

He heard the sounds of passion before he reached the room. He knew what they signified. But who? Who could it be? He moved ever so quietly to the chamber opening and pulled aside the silken covering over the door.

Ping was on his back amid the pillows, arms thrown akimbo over his head, head lolled to the side with a glazed look of deep satisfaction on his face, legs spread wide, and the dark dancer's pelvis between his legs, fucking him with long, strong strokes with that oversized cock of his. Ping had already come—twice—lost in the maddening rubbings of the large gold bar crowing the dancer's cock deep inside his channel.

If he had had a sword, Qiao would have rushed them both and dispatched them there and then. How dare they? Under his roof, under his protection. But just as he was about to burst into the room, there was a dull, panicking thud in his chest. A missing of a beat or a bursting of something? There was no telling, but suddenly Qiao could not breath, and there was a painful pounding in his chest. Instead of confronting the two, he withdrew to his own room and willed himself to be calm and still and to hope that the pain would pass, which, in time it did. Even though he was trying to remain calm, that did not prevent him from thinking. And his thoughts turned to possibilities. The more he thought the more he realized that he could not do without Ping. He could as easily have killed himself as to either kill Ping or lose him. No, life would go on as usual with Ping—as long as Qiao still had life in him. But the dancer. The dancer.

The chamberlain had seen it all. Not only the wild fucking of Ping by the dancer, who the chamberlain himself had led to Ping's room, but the voyeurism of Qiao as well. When Qiao withdrew, so did the chamberlain—a little disappointed that Qiao did not intervene straight away and do what needed to be done, but at least with the knowledge that he had mixed up the relationships inside the house of Deng Qiao. And as long as the relationships were in flux, there was always the possibility that his own position would be enhanced.

Meanwhile, the dancer and Ping fucked on, Ping never before having been taken so vigorously and expertly and with such stamina—meltingly so from one who seemed only a boy—and certainly not with a gold bar caressing every fold deep inside his channel. Ping felt the stirrings of deeper feeling than lust. Ping was beginning to have an inkling of what constituted love.

The only man he had had inside him before now had been Deng Qiao. Ping had had no idea what a young, virile, monster yang chu could do with his arousal and feeling of complete taking. When the dancer disappeared from the household the next day, Ping cursed that he had ever learned what true fucking could be like.

* * * *

It was a great honor—and an opportunity, more than one opportunity Qiao eventually would realize—when the Lord of Shi, ruler of the prefecture Nantung was in, chose to visit the Deng cotton mills. The warrior lord had a considerable army of his own and provided a great opportunity for cotton sales for war tunics for his soldiers. Such a consignment would go overland, and Qiao could avoid risking its seizure by the pirate Ming Lei at the mouth of the Yangtze. It had been fortuitous that the lord had been amenable to an evening's entertainment at Qiao's home after they had toured the busy mills in Nantung.

"It is a daunting task," the lord said with a sigh from the comfort of the pavilion platform's pillows—mellow and relaxed by the proffered food and drink—and not least by the special entertainment that Qiao knew the prince enjoyed when it could be obtained on the sly. They sat back and indulged in the choice tidbits and gazed up at the misty upper reaches of Langshan mountain. Their mood mellowed as they listened to the sweet song and samisen being played in the near distance by Ping, who was artfully positioned on a tatami platform. Royal blue silk skirts billowed around him where he knelt, but his chest and arms were bare. Qiao had purposely had him arranged this way. After having seen Ping's response to his taking by the young down-under dancer and experiencing the singer musician's renewed ardor in the days that followed, Qiao had decided to try to accomplish two desires at the same time.

If the Lord of Shi could be influenced in his cotton buying by the charms of Ping and if Ping were then satisfied by a more virile and satisfying cock than Qiao could provide there would be both rice in the house's bowls and peace in the bed chamber. Qiao, long a secret connoisseur himself, knew of the Lord of Shi's appreciation for the artistic and the exotic and the male.

"A daunting task, you say?" Qiao murmured, hoping he could bring the desultory chat back to cotton cloth.

He was in luck here. "Yes, we have a destiny, you know, Qiao. The campaign of the Kingdom of Wu into that of Chu is doing very well now. And, since young King Jiayi has replaced that old bastard Jili, relations within the land of Wu have also become quite brighter. I have been appointed the quartermaster general of all of the armies of Wu. So, I am not visiting cotton mills only for the needs of the prefecture. I have the army of a kingdom to clothe. From what I can see your mills are very much in contention for the entire contract."

Qiao looked to the lord in interest and ready to form words that would increase the lord's favor toward his mills. The lord wasn't looking at him, though. He was looking and smiling benignly at Ping, who had taken on the look of a frightened deer. Ping was not really frightened, though. He had been coached by Qiao that the Lord of Shi liked his conquests to be innocent—and slightly apprehensive.

The lord sighed heavily as he licked his lips, eyes focused on the graceful and provocative movements of Ping as he strummed his lute and softly sang his song—now appearing to do so directly to the Lord of Shi. "So many soldiers and so much cotton cloth needed for war tunics," the lord said.

"The Deng mills would be honored to serve," Qiao responded in a low, throaty voice. Although disquieted by the thought of Ping being used by another man, Qiao knew such a commission could bring the Dengs back into the highest ranks of favored families of the Kingdom of Wu—and it might also make Ping less restless.

"Yes, such a difficult decision," the lord murmured in a heavy, measured tone.

The Lord of Shi fucked Ping hard and cruelly on the tatami platform, holding Ping crouching on all fours, with his perfectly rounded buttocks orbs lifted, steady with a clutching palm on the little singer's belly, while the lord hunched over his hips and pounded away like he was using a ram to invade the jinan's inner sanctums. And after he'd recovered from his first ejaculation and Ping whimpered softly underneath him, the lord pushed Ping over onto his shoulders and hauled his legs up and fucked down into him again like he was driving a stake into the ground. The lord had a riding crop in his hand and was using it as he would on his war horse when in full pursuit of the enemy.

Ping's body was assaulted and bruised like he was the enemy the Lord of Shi was practicing to defeat, and although Ping cried for mercy, the warrior took no prisoners and gave no quarter. What he gave was a deep drilling inside Ping that was nothing like Qiao was capable of giving, nor did it show any of the concern for Ping's pleasure that the down-under dancer had been careful to provide.

In the darkest hour of the night, Qiao lay on his pallet, listening to the screams emanating from the main pavilion, cries that were a mixture of pain and pleasure, the edges of which the old mill owner could not discern. He regretted the brutality, but he could not pretend that he had not heard that this was the fetish of the Lord of Shi or that he wasn't pleased that Ping was pleasing the man who, potentially, would be the best customer the House of Deng had ever had. Trying not to listen to Ping's pleadings and moans—and to the slapping of the riding crop, Qiao calculated in his mind how many bolts of cotton material it would take to cover the bodies of the soldiers of the army of Wu and how much of this could be delivered by land to avoid the pirate ship of Ming Lei.

The next morning, as Qiao saw off a smiling Lord of Shi—smiling in such a way that the abacus in Qiao's brain was already clacking off potential profit, Qiao found Ping sobbing in his chamber. The master embraced the consort in his arms and rocked him back and forth, but Ping's sobs were inconsolable.

Qiao was having trouble controlling his own emotions as well—and even having trouble discerning all of the conflicting emotions at play. He was sad and distressed. But he was aroused too at the vulnerability and depths of emotion in his young lover.

Ping was in unintentionally fetching dishabille, having not been able to do more than drag himself to his chamber when the Lord of Shi went off to sleep for a few hours before he had to depart. He was clutching the silk skirts he had been wearing on the tatami platform to his bosom, attempting to hide the welts on his chest and thighs, but when Qiao came into the room and gently pulled the silk away to survey the damage, Ping writhed, almost naked, achingly beautiful of body, within the embrace of his master. Miraculously Qiao's cock was hardening, and Ping, knowing his place and also having been strangely aroused by the Lord of Shi's rough play, willingly and fully gave himself to his master, opening his legs, rolling Qiao over on his back and mounting his pelvis, pulling Qiao's cock inside him, and riding him in the undulating movement of a ship on rolling sea. Sobbing away but giving his

83

master full measure of what he had been taken into the household to provide. Qiao raised his lips to Ping's torso and kissed the welts and bruises he found there.

In grateful flow, loving Ping more deeply than ever, Qiao ejaculated what he suspected, from the pounding of his heart, was his last spouting of Deng seed from his loins, all the more moved and appreciative in this revelation.

Holding the trembling Ping in his arms, he whispered, "You are willing to stay with me forever? To be taken to cross over with me, if that is what I desire. And to serve whoever I send you with?"

"Yes, sire. I am yours forever," Ping murmured without hesitation. Ping was recovering from his experience now. And as he recovered, the memory of what the Lord of Shi had done to him adjusted. He would be loyal to Qiao, yes, but now and again he would welcome the variety and danger and ultimate testing that one such as the Lord of Shi could give him.

And Qiao believed his young lover—that Ping would maintain the honor of his position in the Deng household to the death, if necessary, even though his heart might be with another. And very shortly Qiao had to face that reality.

* * * *

One evening, not long after, the first son of Qiao, Longwei—Dragon Greatness—arrived for a visit. This was an unusual occurrence. Longwei was his mother's son, and Qiao was virtually ignoring his first wife. Longwei—and, for that matter, the senior wife Meilin, assumed that Qiao had taken up with concubines in his Nantung retreat. For his part, Qiao did nothing to disabuse his family of that notion, and he kept concubines near him, although it was Ping who slept with him at night—at least until Longwei's unexpected arrival.

Longwei appeared when Qiao was sitting on the summer decking by a waterfall that fell from a steep incline of the looming Langshan and listening to Ping, sitting on a tatami platform, playing his lute and singing a sad song for Qiao.

Fortuitously, Qiao's concubines were gathered about him. Longwei gave his father a nasty stare when he appeared unexpectedly, purposely not announced by the chamberlain, who, when they appeared, was disappointed that Qiao and Ping were not engaging in a lewd act. Qiao just smiled blandly, though, reveling in the knowledge that Longwei could have received a far more shocking sight than concubines fanning their master and rubbing his aching legs with soothing oil.

Ping had fully recovered from his bruising and the welts that the Lord of Shi's riding crop had left on his body, and he was posed just as he had been for the Lord of Shi, swathed from waist down in blue silk skirting, but bare of torso and arms.

The afternoon light was filtering between the trees under the waterfall, with a beam falling full on Ping. Longwei, who was a man who fully appreciated young men, took his breath in sharply when his attention went from his father to that of the singer and lute player.

Neither that effect nor the handsome countenance of Longwei were lost to Ping either. The eldest son was all of the things that Qiao had been thirty years earlier, but that he largely had now lost. He was handsome of face, stood tall and proud, and had the build of a wrestler. Qiao had such length of yang chu that could take pride, even in its withered years. And Ping's first thought was whether the elder son had inherited the father's endowment and whether he was young and virile enough to thicken quickly and to maintain strength.

That night Ping was to find out that the answer to both questions was yes.

Discussion between father and son was polite but strained through the evening meal and the entertainment afterward, with Ping playing the lute and singing and three of the concubines dancing in willowy movements for Qiao and Longwei, who reclined on pillows in the main pavilion overlooking the waterfall.

Qiao was making an effort to show lustful interest in the concubines, determined not to reveal to his family in Gusu that his reasons for separating from them were worse than they imagined. Longwei, however, openly showed interest in Ping.

As they reclined there, Longwei made one last effort to reason with his father for his mother's sake. "You are missed in the capital, Father. The new king of Wu, Jiayi, is open to changing all of the entitlements. He says that the commissioners of his dead father were keeping too much for themselves. We could be negotiating better commissions for the House of Deng."

"We can do that right here, son," Qiao said. "And for that reason it's important that I stay here for a while—and that you work for our family on the Gusu side." He then explained to Longwei the slow but promising negotiations going on with the Lord of Shi for the army cotton material contract. "The quartermaster general for the Kingdom of Wu is here, in the prefecture of Yangzhou, not in the capital. It is here that we will win or lose the best business opportunity we have with the Kingdom of Wu."

"It may take more than favorable purchase terms to achieve a contract in the kingdom, Father," Longwei said. "Perhaps you have been out of the capital too—"

"I know what it takes," Qiao answered with a hard edge to his voice. "It is I who built our family's fortune. Do you not think that I found out the way to the Lord of Shi's good graces? He is a connoisseur of young male flesh—if you can possibly imagine such an inclination. Do you not think Ping, the young man playing so beautifully for us over on the tatami, would appeal to such a man? The Lord of Shi has already visited here and departed quite pleased—and well bribed."

Longwei could not argue about that. Indeed, Qiao could tell the young man didn't want to argue—or even talk with Qiao further. Longwei's full attention had gone to Ping, who had now turned three quarters from the father and son and let the silk skirting drop half way down the line of his buttocks, so that the two men got the full benefit of the curve of Pings back going down to the orbs of his buttocks and the inviting crease in between.

This was enough to put both father and son in full arousal, but only Longwei was able to show that it had. He, though, didn't wish to any more than his father did. Just as the father didn't want to reveal his inclination to the son, the son did not want to reveal his to the father.

"It is getting late, Father, and I have covered a great distance today."

Qiao took that to mean that the son wanted to retire, when, if he had been less concerned with showing interest in the concubines and more concerned with watching his son that evening, he would have understood that Longwei was trying to send Qiao to bed.

Longwei's ploy worked, though. "The chamberlain has shown you your room, Son," Qiao said. "I and the concubines will now go to mine and leave you to get your rest."

"I will go in a few moments, Father," Longwei said. "I have not heard this song before. I would like to hear it to its conclusion."

When the father and concubines were gone, Longwei rose and went to the tatami platform and sat next to Ping.

"That was a new song to me," he said. "It was beautiful, but it was so sad. Do you only play sad songs?"

"Yes, that is all I play," Ping said. His eyes were downcast as he could hardly maintain his steady breath in the presence of this beautiful man. He was sure that if he looked directly into Longwei's eyes, Longwei would know that Ping wanted him to make love to him. He had been told earlier by Qiao to act as if he was an unbitten peach and to say that he was a virgin to men if Longwei asked. Qiao's original intent was to do all he could to keep Longwei from scenting the true reason Qiao wanted to be away from his family. That he had had to reveal that he had let the Lord of Shi use the young musician had changed his original intent. Not having overheard this conversation, though, Ping could not know that he was no longer expected to act the virgin.

"I have tried to learn the lute, but I had trouble with the fingering," Longwei said in a low, husky voice that made Ping melt to him. "Perhaps I was doing it wrong."

"Perhaps," Ping said. "Do you want me to show you the correct positions?"

"Yes, please."

Longwei moved very close to Ping and put an arm around him so that his hands could be next to Ping's as he held the lute and showed Longwei the positions.

Ping realized his hands were trembling. But Longwei's were not. They were strong and steady on the Lute.

"You use a scent in your hair," Longwei whispered. "The fragrance is intoxicating. It gives a man ideas."

"Sire," Ping whispered.

Longwei's lips were at the hollow of Ping's neck and Ping inclined his head seemingly involuntarily, giving Longwei greater purchase there. Longwei took a hand away from the lute, but not the arm embracing Ping, and he untied the sash of his hanfu and pushed the folds of the robes from his body, revealing a long, proud, fully erect cock.

His face still downcast, enabling him to see the richness of Longwei's endowment, Ping murmured, "Sire, I am innocent, unknown by man."

"All the better," Longwei answered in a hoarse voice, enjoying what he now knew was a game, as he had been told that the Lord of Shi had already bitten this peach. But to pretend that Ping was a virgin was more arousing to Longwei than being assured he was. Longwei appreciated experience and skill. "You do not wish to remain that way forever, do you?" As he was saying that, he took Ping's chin in his hand and lifted his head, staring directly into Ping's eyes. He saw there exactly what he had hoped to see. "No, I think not. May I be your first?"

Ping emitted a little whimper but did not answer.

"If no, say no," Longwei whispered. After a moment of silence between them, he murmured, "Thank you."

"I'm afraid," Ping murmured, playing his role to the hilt.

"I will be brave for both of us. Just let me lead you through the gate."

Ping gave a little whimper again. Longwei gently took the lute from his hands and placed it well away from the taking field in the center of the tatami platform. Then he, again gently, pushed Ping down onto his back, ran his hands under the hem of the voluminous skirting and pushed the material up to

88

where it bunched on Ping's chest. He took in his breath noisily when he saw that Ping was naked underneath the skirting—and that his body was perfectly formed.

His mouth lowered to Ping's yang chu and slowly swallowed it down to the root. Ping sighed and set his hips into a slow roll to match the rhythm of Longwei's sucking. Longwei's fingers went to the rim of Ping's opening, and Ping moaned and opened his legs in a wider stance.

When Ping had ejaculated down Longwei's throat, Longwei bent Ping over onto his chest and ran a hand down his back and over the orbs of the young man's buttocks. Longwei was a buttocks man and spent several moments cupping and stroking and separating them. Having pulled them apart, Longwei looked down at the rosebud of an opening between, which Ping was making quiver in such an inviting tease that Longwei's mouth moved to his channel opening. Ping rewarded Longwei's attention there with little moans and sighs, and he rolled his hips in waves, murmuring appreciation of the sensations when Longwei's tongue invaded him.

Longwei turned Ping on his back, and, with Ping lifting his legs over Longwei's shoulders, raised Ping's pelvis to him and returned his attention to the puckered hole as if he were drinking nectar from a cup. Ping dug his hands into the hair on the back of Longwei's head and muttered, "Now, now, now," whereupon Longwei raised up on his knees between Ping's thighs, possessed Ping's mouth with his, and slowly pressed into Ping's channel with his cock. Ping was panting hard and clawing at Longwei's back, using all of the tricks he'd been taught as a jinan to fool a man into thinking he'd been the first.

It was a long journey of Longwei's cock up inside Ping, But when he was fully encased, he disengaged from the kiss. Ping arched his head back toward the tatami mat, with Longwei holding his body steady with a palm of his hand in the small of Ping's back, and Longwei's tongue and teeth went to Ping's pert little engorged nipples.

Longwei began to pump, first in slow, long, steady strokes, and then faster, in off-beat rhythm and stroking that had Ping jerking and then moving his hips, taking control of the stroking, bringing it back in rhythm. He knew how to keep his channel tight on a cock. He also knew how to make his muscles undulate over the cock so that Longwei was getting the loving of his life. Longwei grunted and talked in the language of the gutter of what he was doing to his conquest. Ping moaned and groaned and murmured of being stretched and filled to the limit as he'd been taught to say to clients—but this time meaning it all.

When Longwei ejaculated, Ping cried out, and crossed his legs tightly around Longwei's waist, holding him inside, taking all of the seed Longwei had to give.

In the shadows, the chamberlain watched, smiling and contemplating how he could use this to get rid of the jinan.

Later that night, Qiao rose from his bed and quietly pattered out into the corridor. He could not go a night without attention from his young lover. But when he went to the room formally assigned to Ping, the singer wasn't there. Returning down the corridor, he heard the unmistakable sounds of lovemaking. He peered into the doorway to his son's room.

Ping was laying on Longwei's mat on his belly, and Longwei was stretched out on top of him. Only their hips were moving, but there was no doubt where Longwei's yang chu was churning. The two were kissing, so neither heard Qiao's low gasp or saw the expression of grief and shock on his face.

That night, with his concubines sleeping on mats around his bed, Qiao suffered a heart attack.

It did not kill him, but it was serious enough that Longwei did not leave the next day as he intended. Or at least that was the excuse he used.

Both Longwei and Ping moved around the mansion as if in a cloud of smitten love—all except when either was in the presence of Qiao, commanded by his doctors to remain in his bed.

The two young men fucked whenever and wherever they could.

"You must return to Gusu with me when I leave," Longwei whispered to Ping after a tryst. "I will set you up in your own house. I will give you whatever you want or need. All you have to do is open your legs to me." So taken with Ping was Longwei that he had completely put out of his mind what his father had said about the Lord of Shi being first. Ping had been so much the innocent in Longwei's lovemaking that Longwei had come to think that his father had lied out of pique at being instructed on how to win a government contract.

"You give me by far the easiest duty," Ping said with a small laugh. He didn't say yes to Longwei's proposal, but he was so much in love with the younger version of Qiao that he knew he'd go with Longwei if that's what Longwei wanted, no matter what.

Qiao began to get better, and he got cranky. One night, while Ping was still in the main pavilion, playing a sad song on his lute for Longwei, both waiting for the household to settle so that they could fuck wildly, one of the concubines came to Ping.

"The master is calling for you, Ping," she said. "He wishes you to attend him."

Ping looked over to Longwei.

"You must go," Longwei said. "We have the whole night."

Qiao dismissed the concubines as soon as Ping had entered the room. "I have missed you terribly," he said. He was propped up on pillows in his bed. "I can't go any longer without being inside you."

"But the doctors have said—"

"Bahh to the doctors," Qiao said. "Come sit beside me."

Ping went and sat on the side of the bed. Qiao pulled back the covers and spread his sleeping robe, revealing his withering, but still strong-looking body. His cock was half hard.

"Please."

Ping leaned over and took the old man's cock in his mouth and began to work it. It responded perhaps more strongly than it had for many weeks. Perhaps, Ping thought, it was from the days of abstinence.

Qiao reached over and pulled Ping's hanfu off his shoulders and moved his hand down the hard torso and into the thatch of hair at his crotch. He took Ping's cock in his hand and started to stroke him.

Please let me give him what he wants, Ping prayed to the heavens. He willed his cock to harden. And it started to. He turned his thoughts to the body of Longwei, the young, virile version of Qiao, and he hardened more. He thought of Longwei making strong, deep love to him, and he managed to ejaculate.

Qiao sighed a satisfied sigh. "Please," he said again.

Ping mounted his hips and saddled his channel on the long, now fully erect cock and began to gently ride his master's staff. Qiao sighed and moved his hands lovingly over the curves of Ping's chest and belly, hips, and thighs.

Feeling Qiao getting closer to coming, Ping rode more vigorously. Qiao was burbling with delight, urging Ping to ride harder.

As Qiao came, strongly and profusion, his head rolled to one side, his eyes set in a blank stare, his mouth formed a satisfied smile, and he was dead.

The chamberlain, who was watching from a crack in a door, raised the alarm, and the household gathered in shock and concern in Qiao's bed chamber before Ping could do more than move off Qiao's body. He was in such shock himself that he didn't adjust his hanfu or tie the sash. So, his torso and yang chu were in clear view between the edges of his hanfu when everyone entered the room.

Longwei came into the room, took one look at his father's body and half smiled. Then his gaze went to Ping and the smile froze. He turned and stalked out of the bed chamber.

The chamberlain had Ping locked in a storage room for two days.

When the door was opened after two days, Ping raced to Longwei's room to find the door closed and locked. He beat on it, calling to Longwei to let him in, pronouncing his love for Longwei and not caring who heard.

"He will not hear you," the chamberlain said, with a satisfied smile on his face. "He left to return to Gusu yesterday."

"Left for Gusu? But he was going to take me."

"You cannot go to Gusu," the chamberlain said. "I told him everything of what you were to the old master. You are only going as far as the Cut Sleeve Nanleshijia. The new master of the House of Deng has sold you back to the pleasure house from whence you came."

"You have violated two of the fundamental laws of being a jinan," the chamberlain continued cruelly. "You fell in love with a forbidden man, and you aspired to a position above your station."

"But the inheritance I was to receive—"

Ping went no farther. He could tell by the hearty laugh of the chamberlain that any thought of the promised inheritance was all a dream.

While he was still laughing, the chamberlain grabbed Ping's wrist in strong grip and pulled him farther down the corridor.

"Where?—"

"As part of the sale agreement, Master Longwei granted me a taking."

Ping whimpered but he did not struggle. He knew the chamberlain was right—about both mistakes.

The chamberlain took Ping into Qiao's bed chamber, giggling at the thought of doing it in the dead master's room, on his bed. He pushed Ping down on the edge of the bed; ripped at his robes; quickly revealed Ping's nakedness; and untied his own sash and pulled his robes open. Grabbing Ping's ankles hard enough that Ping winced and called out that there was no need for this, that he wasn't resisting, the chamberlain wishboned Ping legs, moved between his thighs, and stabbed at his hole with a short but thick and hardened cock until he had managed to gain purchase, and then he thrust hard, again and again and again, his hate-driven fucking closer to that of the Lord of Shi than of either Longwei or his father.

Ping turned his eyes to the side and repeated over and over again in his mind that he would never love a man again.

Chapter Seven: Shun and Rong in the Kingdom of Chu

Shun was shuffling along with a line of other young men, all in leg shackles and bound to each other. They had walked, between horsed soldiers of the Chu army, most of the day, with few rest breaks and even fewer stops for water or food. When the line came to a stumbling halt, because a young soldier of Wu was too wounded or weak to go on, he was unshackled from the rest and dragged into the bush at the side of the road. Shun had no idea how these men fared after that.

All of the men taken were young; no grizzled warriors of Wu were in the line of chained prisoners.

He had no idea why he had been taken during the short raid into the encampment of the King of Wu or where they were going. He only knew he needed to continue putting one foot in front of the other, or that he'd be taken into the bush at the side of the road.

His back, under his shoulder blade, where the sword of the horseman had only slightly nicked him, thanks to the pack—as well as Niu's pack—he'd had on his back, was only a dull ache now. That he could endure, and if he ever got back to Niu again, he would not complain about having to carry Niu's pack as well as his own. The wondering of why he'd been spared and then taken in the raid was more of a bother to him than the itchy scratch.

As dusk started to settle into dark, he began to discover more of the why. The line of prisoners was stopped and soldiers of Chu came among them, prodding their bodies and turning them this way and that, looking them over very closely. Five of the smaller, more physically appealing, and well-formed of the young men were unchained and taken aside as the other prisoners were jostled away from the road and up a small hill and forced to squat near the tree line. They were left chained to each other and the chains were secured around thick three trunks. A couple of soldiers were left to guard the prisoners, while most of the rest started to set up a temporary camp and light fires closer to the road.

Five soldiers, however, led the five separated captives, of which Shun was one, up, past the staked-out prisoners and into the forest. The five captives were pushed down unto their haunches beside trees, a separate tree for each, and one of their wrists bound with leather roping, which was passed around the tree trunk and then bound to the other wrist of the prisoner, forcing them on their backs, with their arms raised above their heads.

The soldiers knelt between the spread thighs of the trussed captive of their choice and each did whatever he needed to do to prepare himself for giving and the prisoner for taking.

The soldiers were the senior of the guard; the one who had chosen Shun was the captain of the guard, a grizzled man of advanced age but of heavy musculature that marked him as a man not to be challenged lightly. He had once been a handsome man, but there was an old gash mark that extended from the top of one ear, down his cheek, and over his lips to his chin. It gave him a fierce look, with a mouth whose emotions had been split by the sword, one side smiling and the other side sneering. Shun could not look into the man's face that was hovering just above his while the warrior fucked Shun with a manly cock that knew what it was doing.

The noises Shun heard from the four adjacent trees told him that the other four soldiers were doing the same as the captain.

Even though Shun couldn't stand to watch the captain's face, he intuitively knew that he needed to please this man. This was the captain of the guard, the one who held all of their lives in thrall. Chances were good that none of these five captives would leave the forest alive, but Shun could but try to save himself.

Shun had learned much at the Cut Sleeve Nanleshijia in Nantung while the jinan were training, even though his own training had been cut short. Just as they trained with mainly description and a few equipment aids, so did Shun when he managed to be alone. He knew the sounds to make to tell the man inside him that he was a master, he'd learned the secrets of tightening his channel around a yang chu and making love to it with the muscles of the channel wall, and he learned to arch his back and to praise the fucking and cry out for more, faster when the man was tightening and approaching climax. He knew not to just lay there inertly, but to move his hips in rhythm with the fuck and, at the last moment, to wrap his legs around the waist of his man and hold him deep inside for the clouds and rain—and to tell the man, with feeling, that no other man had touched him this deep and satisfyingly.

He also knew that a man wanted him to signal his own passion by coming first and with cries of passion.

He must have learned well, because when the captain ejaculated inside him after furiously thrusting as if he were still on the battlefield, he remained there, with Shun's legs encasing his waist, panting hard and moving his lips to the hollow of Shun's neck and down to his nipples. When he tongued back up to Shun's face, the young prisoner closed his eyes and let the captain open his lips with his own. Shun sucked on the captain's invading tongue as he had been taught to do to show total capitulation and he began to move his hips again, bringing the captain's yang chu back to strength.

Meanwhile, the four other soldiers had finished, leaving their conquests groaning and whimpering and were replaced by four fresh soldiers, already holding their engorged cocks in their hands, and ready to give the second fucking.

A soldier was standing beside the crouching captain too, but with a gruff command and a flick of his wrist, he waved the soldier away. Soon, though, that soldier returned with another captive in tow, tied him off to another tree, and the chain of five relief stations once more was intact.

But by now the captain's buttocks where moving again, constricting and expanding, as he fucked Shun more slowly and languidly, paying more attention to Shun's prostate with the bulb of his cock, and being rewarded with shuddering and exclamations of ecstasy from Shun.

This time after the captain had come, he moved his knees up to beside Shun's chest and presented his cock for cleaning. "Bite it and you're a dead man," he growled.

Amazingly, after Shun had given him the suck play he wanted, rather than leaving, he moved back down to Shun's hips, encased himself on Shun's yang chu, and slowly rode the young captive's cock, seeming to enjoy having a man inside him as much as he'd enjoyed fucking Shun.

While this was proceeding, Shun turned his face to the side to see how the other captives were faring. Four of them were enduring their third soldier. One of those captives was struggling and cursing—and he was being beaten with the fists of his laughing oppressor for his trouble. Shun did not think he'd survive to his fifth man unless he became wiser and stopped fighting it. Two other captives were laying there like limp rags, softly whimpering, barely conscious. For them, it would be a long night too, Shun thought.

Shun was surprised to recognize that the fifth captive, the one brought up later to substitute for the captain's unwillingness to yield with him, was Rong, the young soldier deflowered by Niu just the previous night. As he was looking at Rong, Rong's face turned to his. It was full of fear and pain and shock.

"Do not fight it, Rong," Shun whispered loud enough for the young soldier to hear. "Think of each one as being Niu and being welcome. Open to it. Do whatever you need do to survive."

The worry began to melt from Rong's face. He had understood. As Shun watched, he saw Rong relaxing, and his hips begin to move. He looked back into the meaty soldier's face that was grimacing down at him—and he smiled. The soldier reacted with surprise and new ardor. He lowered his lips to Rong's, and Shun noticed that his buttocks lost the sharp, rapid movement of the rough fuck and that he was taking it slower now.

Rong would manage, Shun thought. Just as Shun would do whatever he had to do to keep the captain of the guard happy.

When both Shun and the captain were spent with the captain riding Shun's cock, the solider laid his barrel chest on Shun's and looked down into his face. Shun could look at him directly now. He knew he had to learn to do this without wincing, and he had to admit that he was enjoying the cocking. The captain did not have the length and thickness and power of Niu's cock, but at least he seemed to recognize that Shun was there, which was not something Niu did well unless he wanted a favor. Although it had started off as only the captain's pleasure, it had become the two of them working together for mutual pleasure.

"You pleasure me," the captain said—saying it almost as if it was an unexpected surprise.

"You pleasure me as well," Shun said with a smile on his face. "Please, will you fuck me again?"

Of all the tricks Shun had learned in the nanleshijia, this was the most important. Even if the client is paying grandly for the use of your channel, tell him you want another ride. He will feel a man. He likely will be willing to pay even more the next time.

"In a moment, my little bird," the captain said. "And there will be more tonight. You will sleep on my mat tonight. You are not a stranger to this, are you?"

"No, sire," Shun answered. "I am not a soldier. I was a jinan—male prostitute—for the court of the Wu. I have worked in a male house of pleasure—in Nantung. The famous

Cut Sleeve Nanleshijia. If you unbind me and keep me with you, I can make love to your yang chu in the manner that is fit for a king."

Shun was pulling out all stops. He was sure that a soldier of Chu would be proud to be mining a channel that the royals of the House of Wu had dipped in. It didn't matter that it wasn't true. That he had been a mere servant, not a trained jinan in the nanleshijia. This was a matter of survival, and Shun very much doubted that the captain of Chu had the least notion of what a male courtesan could do.

Indeed, this information seemed to arouse the captain. Shun could feel the man's cock hardening on his stomach.

Much as the captain was aroused at sharing a channel with the King of Wu, though, he seemed to have a greater interest in something else Shun had mentioned. "You worked in a famous nanleshijia, did you say?"

"Yes, my lord. You are magnificently strong and built like a horse, so I could show you the position of the galloping—"

"You know the workings of a nanleshijia? The management?"

"Yes, of course. Does that—?"

"You could manage a nanleshijia for me, then? That is what our charge is. We were to bring young, comely men of Wu back from this raid. The army of Chu wants to establish a nanleshijia for its officers on the shores of Tai Hu Lake—outside the capital at Danyang. The court wants nothing of that sort inside the capital city, so I must set one up at Tai Hu."

"Yes, I could do that," Shun said. He moved the heels of his feet to the muscle of the captain's calves and started to massage his legs. There was so much more Shun could do to keep the captain's ardor up—to make him believe that Shun wanted him—if he could get his hands free. He began to willfully tremble and to sigh and to give the captain "now, again . . . please" looks.

He believed he may be coming out of this well enough. But now he thought of the others—and especially of Rong, who was being taken by his third soldier, who wanted to stand, feet planted firmly in the ground and hold the pelvis of the diminutive Rong to his crotch with strong hands on Rong's waist, and while Rong was arched back to toward the ground, pull the youth's body back and forth on his cock. Rong was giving Shun a plaintive "just barely enduring it look."

There were strangled whimperings and manly grunts coming from Shun's other side and he turned his head to see that an arriving soldier would not wait for the one before him to be finished with one captive and that they were sharing the captive's hole.

"We could open a nanleshijia with these young men, sire—your soldiers have picked candidates well. But the strength of a nanleshijia in Wu is in providing virgins. May I suggest that—?"

"Virgins?" the captain exclaimed. "What an idea. A man of Chu wants his jinan experienced and well used. The men of Chu are magnificently endowed; we want holes that will take us easily. What my men are doing here is beginning the preparation of making these captives into the holes that the soldiers of Chu want to dip in."

"But these captives up here, sire. Some will not live the night. Few will want to poke dead men."

"There are more staked below," the captain growled. "How many jinan do you need for a nanleshijia?"

The captain was getting irritated, and Shun didn't want to lose him. He started moving his belly so that the underside of the captain's cock was rubbing against it. Shun started to pant and moan. He moved his pelvis so that the captain's cock slipped under his balls and the bulb was rubbing against the rim. With all of the concentration he could manage, Shun got the cap of the cock positioned up against his hole and he started puckering the rim against the bulb.

"Now. please . . . don't make me wait longer," he murmured in a breathy voice.

Also with hoarse voice, the captain whispered. "How do you want it, little bird? This one is for you."

"Hard and furious," Shun cried out. "Be a soldier. Conquer me."

It must have been what the captain wanted to hear, because he laughed heartily and gave Shun what he asked for.

And this time it was the captain who was the more winded and exhausted of the two after the climax.

"One favor?" Shun asked as they were cooling down.

"I will not unbind you until we reach Tai Hu Lake," the captain answered.

"Not that. To manage a proper nanleshijia, I will need an assistant. Someone I can trust. I know that captive over there. His name is Rong. May I have him—alive and unruined—as my assistant?"

* * * *

Within weeks Shun had set up a nanleshijia for the army of Chu in a many-pavilioned compound that was provided by the army on a cliff overlooking Tai Hu Lake. The villa was nothing like the Cut Sleeve Nanleshijia. It was more like an army barracks. And the soldiers coming here for sexual relief were nothing like the refined clients Shun had known in Nantung. They were rough and brutal. Shun quickly learned why they wanted their jinan well used and toughened to the cock—they wanted them to survive to the point of ejaculation.

The captain stayed with Shun and in his bed—being lost to Shun as Shun knew he would be once Shun had the use of his hands and could make love to the captain in all of the ways Shun had seen practiced in the Cut Sleeve pleasure house. But it wasn't more than a couple of weeks before the nanleshijia was so popular that the captain had to take to the field again with most of his soldiers to recruit new jinan.

Guards were left at the nanleshijia, though, and although Shun started to plan an escape for Rong and himself almost from the time the captain first told him of the plans to establish a nanleshijia, the guards were still too much on the alert and Shun hadn't managed to scrape together enough of the means to escape or to have been able to slowly extract from people around him how far it was back to Wu territory and what the best avenues of escape were. Shun didn't have a clue where he was in relationship to a border of Wu, for that matter.

The longer Shun went without escaping, the harder it became for him to want to. He found that he enjoyed being the zhaoguzhe—caretaker—of a nanleshijia house. Or he would enjoy it immensely if it was one set up to service the pleasures of the refined gentlemen of Wu rather than the coarse soldiers of Chu. However, whenever he thought of just settling where he was and being content with the man who had saved his life, his thoughts went to wondering what had happened to Niu. He could not deny his addiction to Niu no matter how attentive to his sexual needs the captain was. And when he thought of Niu, he thought of Nantung and pined to be there.

Shun did his best for the jinan and was sorry to see the captives slowly disappear or die, but he took heart that the captain had permitted him to keep Rong by his side untouched—at least to the extent that Rong wanted to be untouched.

Rong had gotten a taste for the yang chu. Shun enjoyed a good ride himself, but as long as the captain was there, he was getting quite enough of that. Rong wanted the attention and was learning the wiles of seduction and holding the interest of a man from Shun, but whenever he'd gone with one of the soldiers sent to the nanleshijia for relief, he spent several days in the sickbed, unable to close his legs.

There must be some middle ground, Shun thought.

It was Rong who gave Shun an idea of this middle ground. There were tradesmen who brought supplies to the nanleshijia, and it was Rong who was assigned to receive these supplies and pay the tradesmen. One day after Shun had seen the exchange of vegetables for money, Rong left the kitchens with the tradesman and didn't come back for some time. When he did, Shun could hear the clinking of coins in Rong's hand, and the young man went directly to his room. The next time Shun saw him leave with a tradesman, he followed at a distance. When he got out to the entrance court to the nanleshijia, he saw no sign of Rong or the tradesman. So, he walked down the road several paces to where it wound into a copse of trees. There he saw that the tradesman's now-empty cart was drawn up to the side of the path. Empty of vegetables now, that is. The tradesman was leaning over the open tail of the cart, his back toward Shun, and the ankles of Rong's bare legs were hung on his shoulders on either side of his head.

Shun could have been angry that the nanleshijia's money was going into Rong's pockets soon after it was given to tradesmen, but he wasn't. The nanleshijia was getting its vegetables. And watching the tradesman fuck Rong, and listening to his pleasure in doing so, told Shun that there were randy men to be served in the local community who would pay for it.

So, before the captain left again, Shun got him to agree to devote a section of the pleasure house to civilian men from the vicinity, to be serviced in a more civil style than the soldiers wanted. The captain had reluctantly agreed, but he'd questioned whether there was demand for such services. When he found that there was high demand among the local men, he then objected on the grounds that he wasn't going to raid for captives to serve anyone but the armymen for whom they were intended.

"We will find young men to serve just this section of the house, then," Shun said. "Young virgins we can sell at high—?"

"No virgins," the captain had blustered. "I've told you that the men of Chu want experienced jinan."

Having gained permission for a separate section of the house, Shun did not want to press his luck on the virgin issue, so he decided to save that for another day. "I'm not sure then how we will obtain jinan," he said. "In Wu we train them up from their early years."

"Why, we'll contract a *zhaodaojen*—procurer—then," the captain had said—as if Shun should know what a zhaodaojen was. But when Shun looked at him with confusion, he patiently explained. "We have nanleshijia in the capital, Danyang, too—mostly for the court. And they use the services of a zhaodaojen. A zhaodaojen buys appropriate young men— usually from poor parents—and prepares them for service as a jinan and sells them to the nanleshijia when they are properly trained. We have such zhaodaojen here at the lake. Most of them are boatmen with pleasure boats. They break young men

103

and then take them to the capital. That is where the nanleshijia were centered before the army decided to set one up here."

"So they don't come as virgins?" Shun asked, incredulous. "The zhaodaojen uses the most expensive service of a jinan?"

"I have said to forget this virgin nonsense," the captain said in exasperation. "The men of Chu want their jinan experienced and will slack holes to take our yang chu."

"We would have to find and contract one of these zhaodaojen then?" Shun said. He just could not believe that the captain had this right.

But so exasperated was the captain now that he went down to the lake himself. When he returned, he brought two men before Shun, one a solid, handsome man of rough demeanor and the other a young man so beautiful that Shun would not have doubted him if he said he was from Nantung, which was renowned for its beautiful young men.

"This is Wangtao," the captain said, indicating the older man. "He is a boatman, but he is a zhaodaojen too. He supplies nanleshijia in Danyang, but I have paid him to supply to us as well."

"And who is this?" Shun asked, placing his hand on the arm of the younger man and pulling him forth into the light. He was shy, and Shun's first instinct was to think that the captain had everything all wrong and that he was a virgin as well. The sale of his innocence would bring the nanleshijia quite a tidy fortune, Shun thought, and his mind was already racing on who in the area of Tai Hu Lake would be interested in bidding.

"Wangtao poles a pleasure boat on the Danyang Lakes," the captain continued. "I have convinced him that business will be better here on Tai Hu Lake, though, and he has agreed to work with the nanleshijia, and we will include pleasure cruises on his boat in our services."

"This is Pai," Wangtao spoke for the first time. "I have prepared him for jinan."

Shun looked at the rough boatman and then at the beautiful, lithe Pai, sure that "prepared" for Wangtao meant something different from what it meant for the captain. But then his thoughts were arrested. Pai was looking at Wangtao with a look in his eyes that Shun had seen before. Yes, he thought, somewhat bitterly, not only does this youth admire and love this brute of a boatman, but he has lain under him as well. No doubt the boatman has a magical yang chu that can entrap foolish younger men. I have seen enough of this to know what has gone between them. This young Pai is so smitten that if the zhaodaojen asked him to lay down here and open his legs to both him and the captain at the same time, the youth would do it.

It was hard for Shun to countenance, but he could not deny it was true.

Shun sighed and looked upon Pai with concern as the captain struck the deal with Wangtao for Pai's services as a jinan. In the bargain, however, Wangtao was to remain Pai's handler and Wangtao and Pai would ply their trade on Tai Hu Lake rather than in the capital.

This can only end in tragedy, Shun thought. He would have preferred to separate the two and take Pai directly into the nanleshijia. One of the basic laws of the jinan is not to fall in love. And especially not to do so with someone in the business rather than some rich old and sick man who can leave you both rich and young. But this was the arrangement the captain had struck, and Shun decided he needed to take baby steps in establishing this procurement process.

Shun could hardly wait to be alone with Pai to satisfy his curiosity on where such a beautiful young man came from, what brought him here, and how he had come to love the man who had debauched and sold him.

When he had heard the story, he was not surprised, but he was very sad. And he was even sadder when he had to experience what subsequently happened to Pai's love.

Chapter Eight: The Bridge of Sighs

The music made Pai smile. He had heard the sweet song of Wangtao, the handsome stranger from Danyang his father had met at the Dan River ferry stand, many times before in the brief time Wangtao had been in the village, but now it was bringing tears to his eyes. He could not be sure why, but he was trembling, knowing that something momentous was happening. Or perhaps it was the drink. He hadn't had so much wine in all of his years. The rice wine, the *chiu*, was bitter at first, but the more he drank, the smoother tasting it became—and the more it relieved him of his trembling and the more it heated his body. The meltingly attractive Wangtao— many years older than he was and hardened from plying a pleasure boat on Tai Hu Lake near Danyang was handsome and strong-bodied—and, to Pai's village sensibilities, urbane. And indeed Wantao was not from the hard-scratch Dan River valley, beaten down alternately by flood and drought. He was here because some of the most handsome men of the kingdom came from this region.

It was hot in the room cut out of the cave high above the trickle of the Dan, in drought these past four years. The air was not moving, and the chiu was heating Pai's body. He loosened the sash of his cotton long coat, his *ta ao*, the most formal and dear clothing that his teary-eyed *mu chin* and *fu chin* had insisted he take away from his home with him on this momentous day, and pulled the edges of the crinkly material from his chest.

Wangtao leaned into him and pulled the garment completely off his shoulders. It fell around Pai's waist where he knelt before the low table just inside the shadows of the cave room entrance. Incense was burning on the table, sending wafts of smoke spiraling up the uneven rock ceiling, blackened by centuries of cooking fires.

Pai began to shake and wrapped his arms around his chest, but Wangtao smiled at him and, in a tender gesture, reached over and placed the palm of his hand on Pai's sternum and ran it up between Pai's trembling chest and his forearms. Pai dropped his arms and Wangtao gently ran long, strong, callused fingers across Pai's chest, following the well-muscled folds and circling the nipples, which went erect as a chill ran down Pai's spine. Wangtao had told him he had a beautiful body. The girls of Zigui had always told him this as well. But this was the first time an important visitor from a sophisticated city had said this to him—almost as if he was worth more than a life in Zigui.

As if to convey that everything was all right, Wangtao smiled at Pai again and pulled the sash on his own robe and shrugged it off his shoulders so that the folds descended on and mingled with the coarse cotton of Pai's ta ao. Wangtao's robe was of much finer material than Pai's was, as was in keeping with Wangtao's greater sophistication and position in the world. He was from Danyang. A pleasure barge master of the Danyang Floating World.

Pai knew this. Wangtao's seduction was one of several weeks, but Pai had not been misled. Pai's mu chin and fu chin had not been misled. Some things were inevitable. The pitiful trickle of water in the Dan determined many things that just were to be.

Wangtao sang softly to Pai. His voice was rich and haunting. It served him well down in Danyang, where he sang when poling his pleasure barge on the lakes in the Floating World district while his clients were being entertained on the silken pillows in the barge's belly.

Pai was so warm that he moved to rise and stand for a few moments in the twilight at the entrance of the cave room to take in the evening breeze, but the chiu was making him clumsy, and he slipped and would have fallen back off the matting onto the rock floor if Wangtao hadn't quickly leaned over and encircled the youth's shoulders in his strong arms.

He was looking down into Pai's face with that handsome, searching, reassuring smile of his. He was humming the melody of his signature pleasure barge poleman song to the one he had chosen to return to Danyang with him—to be prepared to serve in a nanleshijia, a men's pleasure house. Wangtao had already spoken to Pai of this, painting the Floating World of Danyang as a paradise, and Pai had believed it was a paradise compared to the life he lived here in his village. Wangtao had told him that out of a bit of pain there arose a world of pleasure. And Pai, already in love with Wangtao, believed and trusted the older man.

Pai lay, shoulders arched back, in Wangtao's arms. Knowing what came next, even though he had never done this before. Both welcoming and fearing it. He knew it led to Danyang, away from this impoverished village, made too small for all of the generations here by the fickleness of the river that had always been the center of his life, the Dan. By the river's failure to support the necessary harvests. And the greatest fear—that to follow the drought would be a flood, scouring away the very life of the village, its soil.

The young man shivered as Wangtao's fingers slowly glided down from his chest, across his belly, and unknotted his *tuan ku*. The ends of the loin cloth fell away, and Pai gave a little lurch as Wangtao's fingers encircled his virgin staff.

Wangtao's lips came down on Pai's, and the youth opened to him and sighed and moaned and moved from fear and trepidation to greater heat and exhilaration, as Wangtao began to slowly pump his fist on Pai's yang chu. Pai initially was restless and instinctively struggled against his heavenly tormentor. But he had known this was coming; he had wanted this. Wangtao was strong and handsome and urbane. And Wangtao had told him of all of the glories of Danyang—in terms that made it very clear to Pai where his opportunity lay in becoming a part of Danyang. And Pai desperately wanted to be in Danyang—and to be away from the shriveling Zigui.

And, Aeiiii, Pai had had no idea that it could be like this. He had, of course, pleasured himself in the darkness of his own family's cave room corners. But now he had no control. He could not rest. He could not pace himself; this was being done by another, entirely in the control of another. The rubbing and rhythmic pulling of his yang chu was relentless. Pai groaned and tried to beg for mercy through the possessive kiss of Wangtao, whose tongue had fully invaded Pai's mouth and was swabbing his inner cheeks and reaching along the roof of his mouth to the back of his throat. Darting and rubbing. Pulling Pai's own tongue into his mouth and sucking it.

And Wangtao's big, strong, callused hand pulling on Pai's yang chu. His thumb playing in the precum-slathered slit in the yang chu's bulging head.

Pai began to move his hips, to the extent that Wangtao's firm grip allowed. Rising and falling. Wangtao loosening his grip on the yang chu, providing a sleeve for Pai to move in, rhythmically, insistently.

Pumping, pumping, pumping. Skin sliding against skin.

Wangtao released Pai's mouth and moved his lips and teeth down to the erect nubs on Pai's hard, shuddering chest, as the youth threw his head back and concentrated his gaze on the incense trails curling up to the blackened ceiling. Wangtao was bringing his signature tune to a conclusion.

With that, Wangtao bit lightly down on Pai's nipple, and the youth cried out to the streams of upward spiraling smoke. His hips lurched, and he sprayed his youthful seed up onto his tight, quivering belly.

Preparation lesson one completed.

* * * *

When he first visited Pai's hut, Wangtao had said it was called becoming a cut sleeve. Mu chin and fu chin had understood service in the Floating World well enough—they had sold Pai's sisters into that world already. But, simple as they were, they had had no idea that a comely son would have value of this kind as well. They needed the money for the family to survive the Dan's drought, which was sure to be followed by a flood. That was for sure; it was the time-worn cycle of life along the Dan. But when they had parted with their daughters, they had done it more for their benefit, the selling of the daughters into the Floating World. Luckily Pai's family members were blessed with beauty, perfectly formed bodies, straight backs and teeth, and melodious voices. So, they were their own resource and treasure. So many families in Zigui did not have even that, even though the village was legendary for its comely folk. Many of them would not survive to the next killing flood.

The Floating World was a world of comparatively unbelievable wealth. If the daughters had stayed here, they probably already would have starved. If Pai did not somehow leave, he would surely drown in the inevitable flood that would follow the drought. The parents accepted the inevitability of their fate. They were village born and bound and would remain here, accepting whatever the Dan had to give them, no matter what.

Wangtao, handsome and worldly, and relatively wealthy, was an answer to the family's dream. And mu chin and fu chin didn't even have to face the decision of sending their second son into the Floating World in whatever way they could. Wangtao had found and cultivated Pai. Wangtao was a zhaodaojen—a procurer for the nanleshijias of Danyang, and he wished to ply his trade on Tai Hu Lake, near the capital, as well during the resort season there. He had come to Zigui explicitly to find a new cut sleeve youth, having heard that this region up the Dan from Danyang produced likely youths. And Pai had been the most comely of those Wangtao had considered and he had decided he wanted him for service on his new Tai Hu Lake pleasure barge.

For his part, Pai had been smitten by Wangtao and only briefly recoiled from what Wangtao openly and honestly offered him. Smitten won out over the fears of the actual service and was only heightened by the description of Danyang and the Floating World life. Pai had visions of his days in his rich, sophisticated, handsome lover's arms—visions of pleasure that completely obliterated his evenings in his thoughts.

Thus, when Wangtao approached mu chin and fu chin, it was with a willing and beaming Pai at his side.

Pai's parents welcomed the offer as now at Least Pai would survive and might even flourish—and he might, like his sisters, occasionally send something home to help undergird the family and see it through the endless cycle of drought and flood.

* * * *

Wangtao had been as gentle and careful in the initiation as he could be. But that first journey beyond the curtain is never easy.

"Aeiii," Pai moaned, as he tried to spread his legs even farther apart. Wangtao had promised pleasure following pain. And they had yet to come to the promised paradise.

Wangtao was crooning softly in his rich, baritone voice to Pai, while the youth stared down over the lip of the rocky ledge beyond the cave room entrance, down into the Dan gorge at the bare trickle of water wending down toward the desired Danyang. Pai had asked if they could drag the bamboo chair over and do it at the mouth of the cave room, so that he could look down on what this meant he could leave behind. He had told his mu chin and fu chin that he was sure this was what he wanted—and he knew that Wangtao was the one he wanted—but he found he needed this reassurance himself upon jumping that chasm. He needed to concentrate on the reality that Zigui was not a possibility while he was spanning that chasm.

Pai thought the pain was about over, but it was just starting. Wangtao's hand was slathered in the peach butter that he was working between Pai's nether cheeks while the youth was bent over the bamboo chair and gripping its rungs on either side under the straw seat cushion. Wangtao had two fingers working inside Pai, but Pai was already tensing up and groaning and starting to writhe under the onslaught, the aroma of peach butter forever now engrained on his soul as connected with the taking.

"Aeiii!"

"Relax, my little one," Wangtao murmured from behind his bent-over protégé. "It will be well if you let yourself loosen up. Look down there. Look down in the chasm. This is what you are leaving."

Once again Wangtao was singing his signature boatman song, the song he sang as he poled his pleasure barge around the Danyang Lakes, the song by which his clients identified where he was headed and where in the Floating World of Danyang they could move to meet up with what he could provide them.

Pai felt the firm grip on his hips. Holding him fast and pulling his plump cheeks apart.

"Aeiiii!" Pai screamed. It was too large; it would split him asunder. Pai tried to collapse; he tried to struggle away. But the older, stronger Wangtao had him imprisoned with his big, callused fists and was poling ever more deeply inside him with his throbbing yang chu. The master poleman—of boat and of men.

Pai writhed and whimpered and cried out under the grip of Wangtao as the pleasure boatman initiated his protégé into the cut sleeve life.

"Shih. Shih. Yes, yes, just like that. Each and every one who rides you," Wangtao panted out and he relentlessly drove up into his tasty virgin morsel. "Cry for each one as if he is the first lover, just like that. Shih. Shih. Our fortunes will be made."

Pai's eyes watered, and he focused hard on the trickle of water that was the mighty Dan, muttering to himself over and over of how the river had failed his family and how he would not be defeated by it. Wangtao had bottomed his pole inside him now and was withdrawing and advancing, withdrawing and advancing. Pai's knees like rubber, the rungs of the bamboo chair snapping under his white knuckled grip. Wangtao holding him in a strong, pinching grip of the hips.

Wangtao panting and groaning. Pai crying and moaning, but subsiding into whimpers from exhaustion and from new sensations. The pain indeed, as promised, translating itself into new sensations.

He was being taken by his lover. He was one now with his master. Pai began to move with the rhythm of Wangtao's pistoning pelvis. He turned his head, and Wangtao found his lips and devoured him. Not just animals taking. Lovers giving and receiving.

The bamboo chair lost its purchase on the slippery rock floor as Wangtao lowered the weight of his heaving chest on Pai's back and reached his lips to Pai's. The chair skittered out onto the ledge, and Pai saw it career over the edge and crack with an echo once, twice, thrice, as it bounced down the cliffside into the Dan gorge. Pai's life in Zigui also crashing, echoing its demise. His innocence shattered like the delicate chair smashed against the rocks.

Wangtao caught Pai under the armpits before the youth fell to the floor, kicked the mat by the table over underneath Pai, and slowly lowered him to the mat. All without losing the saddle of his long, hard yang chu poling the virgin depths. Wangtao pressed Pai's chest down onto the matting with a big fist in the small of his back. Then he pulled the youth up on his knees, his hips encased between the master's heavily muscled thighs; and continued fucking, fucking, fucking.

Pai closed his eyes and moaned and sighed for his urbane Danyang lover while Wangtao went back to singing his song on the pleasure barge.

The two cried out in unison in their finishing as Wangtao released deep inside Pai and Pai gave up his youthful seed inside Wangtao's fist.

"Shih. Shih," Wangtao whispered in Pai's ear after kissing him on the cheek. "*Hen hao*. Very good. Very, very good. Each time. Give that each time with the men on the pleasure barge, and I will be very pleased."

Preparation lesson two completed.

Pai exalted. He had pleased his lover. He could hardly hold back the tears. The pain was worth it. He would run and pack now, and . . .

"We rest for a few minutes," Wangtao said, standing up and giving Pai a hardy slap on the rump. "Then we will go to the mat and I will show you a favorite position in Danyang, the dog in heat. Later I will bed you and teach you the holing of the snake position."

* * * *

Wangtao was nothing if not fully attentive and assiduous in his methodical training and preparation of Pai. He was not always this attentive of his trainees, but there had been no earlier trainee that Wangtao so much wanted to sheath his yang chu.

He was standing at the entrance of the cave, staring into the starry night over Pai's shoulder. This was the strong man chair position, he had whispered to Pai. While Wangtao stood, with legs slightly spread to give him balance, Pai was suspended in front of him, also facing out into the night, impaled on Wangtao yang chu. His legs were spread, supported by Wangtao's outstretched arms, and his own arms were raised, with his fists clinched behind Wangtao's neck. Movements of Wangtao's arms were making Pai's channel rise and fall and move back and forth on the impaling staff. Pai moaned at the deep taking.

The blue of the night sky beyond the blackness of the cave was lightening as Pai slowly awoke to the hot breath of Wangtao on his neck. The young man was pinned to his pallet on his belly by the weight of the heavier man. Pai winced as Wangtao's yang chu slowly worked its way into his channel. Then he gasped when Wangtao grabbed his wrists, raised up to a kneeling position between his thighs, and pulled Pai's chest off the pallet in a taut arch. As Wangtao started to rock Pai's body back and forth on his buried cock, he whispered, "The position of the tight bow."

They lay, panting, both spent, as dawn crept over the lip of the cave and pushed the darkness deeper into the cavern beyond Pai's pallet.

"When you have rested a bit, I believe you may be ready for the position of the heavenly sling."

* * * *

The cock was short but thick, and the fat merchant was bellowing his well-invested lust as Pai swallowed his yang chu whole, ingested his balls as well, and sucked them into his cheek cavities. He was humming, just as Wangtao had taught him to do with the small-membered clients, and the merchant was beside himself in the sensation of the warm, moist sheath and the vibrations from the humming. The client was flopping like a landed fish underneath Pai amid the pile of pillows in the center of the pleasure barge Wangtao was poling across the Tai Hu Lake toward the Bridge of Sighs leading into yet another lake.

The merchant lost control, tearing at Pai's hair with one claw and wrapping his beefy legs around the youth's head, pulling him as close into his groin as possible—loving the full engorgement of his privates into that warm, vibrating chamber. His other claw was ripping at Pai's brocaded hanfu—robe. Wangtao broke off in his singing and poling ever so briefly as the ripping of the fabric harmonized with the merchant's exclamations of lust against the background of the tinkling instruments and voices gliding across the shimmering water from the other floating world pleasure barges.

Then Wangtao shrugged and dug his pole into the muck of the shallow lake's bed once more and propelled the barge toward the three arches of the gracefully upcurved Bridge of Sighs.

Overcome with desire for the impossibly winsome youth in the red brocade robe, the merchant reared up from the cushions and rolled over on top of Pai.

"*Ching . . . pu. Ching . . . pu*! Please, no!" Pai pled in his most pleading voice and struggled—purposely ever so weakly and ineffectively—as the merchant rolled between his spread

115

legs, held the youth's wrists in one beefy fist above his head, plunged his other hand under Pai's buttocks, and dug his fingers into the youth's hole.

"Aeiii! No, please. *Hen da, hen da.* Too big," Pai moaned, further inflaming his client to prodigious power. Seemingly struggling against the merchant, Pai actually dug his heels into the cushions and raised his pelvis to just the right angle for entry.

Feeling his power and skill and cleverness as a lover triangulate, the merchant took advantage of Pai's "mistake" at raising his hips to lodge his yang chu at Pai's opening. Pai writhed and groaned, pleading for mercy and yelping convincingly as the bulging head of the merchant's yang chu breached his anal ring. And it wasn't all for show. The merchant's yang chu made up in thickness now what it lacked in length.

Pai cried and panted as the tool worked inside his hole, tightened to the extent he could now do through the "presenting the virgin" channel muscle exercises Wangtao had taught him in the spring.

As it turned out, Shun was more right than the captain had been. Some clients in the kingdom of Chu *did* want a virgin. Pai's virginity had been paid for several times, and Shun's "escape" fund was building nicely.

By design and excellent training, the "ravaged" youth slowly metamorphosed into the won-over lover, and Pai laid back, arched his back, and raised his hips to the pounding of the transported merchant client's yang chu at his forbidden entrance, as he brought the merchant's lips and teeth to his quivering breast.

Keeping one eye on the client and the jinan, Wangtao poled and sang his signature tune to the sounds of the muffled sucking at Pai's breast and slapping of belly and thighs against belly and groin. Pai hummed along with Wangtao's tune and raised his eyes to the underbelly of the Bridge of Sigh's middle arch, as the pleasure barge moved under the bridge from the larger Tai Hu to the smaller Meihan Lake and the view of mud bricks opened up into the vast array of stars in the clear eastern China summer night sky.

Surely this was the last client of the night. Surely he and Wangtao could now retire to Wangtao's small room at the nanleshijia and it would be for Wangtao that Pai would be spreading his legs and raising his buttocks to receive the unrehearsed, unfeigned deep fucking from Wangtao's, the master poleman's, amazing yang chu that Pai lived for.

* * * *

The spring of Pai's preparation by Wangtao, during which the youth fell fully under the spell of the handsome pleasure barge poleman, had turned into a cut sleeve perfection of summer on the shimmering Tai Hu Lake.

No matter what Pai had had to feign and endure with the evening clients on Wangtao's Floating World pleasure barge, throughout the warm summer, Wangtao took Pai to his bed when they returned to their room in the nanleshijia and plowed him deep and long, and with the ardor that made Pai understand that all that was transpiring in their life together was so that the two could be together as lovers—and that made Pai never even think of leaving Wangtao.

It was unusual for a nanleshijia to permit a jinan to be so coupled with a pleasure house employee, but, being convinced that Pai was so in love with Wangtao that it was only this love that kept him satisfied in the pleasure house where his services increasingly were being sought, the zhaoguzhe, Shun, tolerated the arrangement. At the same time, he often felt sad, believing that Pai's love would someday crumble and destroy him.

Eventually the coolness of the autumn was upon the lakes. Pai now shivered inside his torn red brocade robe when clients were fumbling within its folds and an unexpected breeze fluttered across the water. And coolness came upon Wangtao too. They didn't make love every morning upon returning from the lake as they originally had, and the rhythm of the life they were settling into was not one of red-hot ardor, but more one of domestication, habit . . . and a bit of dullness.

And increasingly it was some other man who was plunging his yang chu inside Pai's undulating channel, as the popularity of the sweet young jinan increased.

Wangtao was consulting with Shun about procuring his next jinan for sale to the nanleshijia, or, rather Shun was saying that another jinan need be procured and Wangtao was not showing enthusiasm. It seemed, Shun thought, that Wangtao had grown as complacent with his husbanding of Pai as Pai was of being coupled with Wangtao.

But the civilian side of the pleasure house on Tai Hu Lake was increasing in demand, and Shun would like to close out the military side when he could as he could not bear to know about the rough demands the soldiers made on the captives the captain supplied with his raids on the Kingdom of Wu.

Pai sometimes overheard bits and pieces of these discussions, but he was innocent to Wangtao's zhaodaojen business in this regard. He did not know that he was only one in a succession of jinan Wangtao had procured and trained. He assumed that Wangtao loved him as he loved Wangtao.

Pai's first thought that he was losing Wangtao came the late autumn afternoon he had been sent out to do marketing and had come right back to the nanleshijia because he had forgotten to take the money—the chi'en—that he needed.

When he drew close to the nanleshijia, he saw Wangtao out on the lake dock below the pavilions of the pleasure house. He was talking with a young man—certainly younger than Pai was. They had their heads together, and the young man was holding a length of the most beautiful scarlet brocade Pai had ever seen.

A chill raced down Pai's spine, and he instantly remembered a conversation he had had with Wangtao shortly after they had come to Tai Hu Lake.

"You came to Tai Hu to your own pleasure barge and to acceptance in the Floating World here, master," Pai had murmured one morning as Wangtao held him still from behind, all in stillness except for Wangtao's masterful yang chu working in and out of Pai's love hole.

"Shih. Shih. Yes, I did," Wangtao said through teeth working their way across Pai's shoulder.

"It does not seem easy to gain position in the Floating World," Pai had whispered.

"Pu yao, No, it's not," Wangtao answered, as he moved his lips from Pai's shoulder and nuzzled his face up into Pai's arm pit, while the youth raised his arm and emitted a low moan at the effect of Wangtao's tongue and teeth on his sensitive flesh there. "I have been a pleasure boatman for many years."

"And you must have had many youths such as me entertaining the men's yang chu's then," Pai had murmured, not believing it, but wanting to hear it denied.

"Shih, Many. But none as fine as you, of course." Wangtao had moved his mouth to the youth's nipple and was sucking it hard between his teeth.

"Aeiii," Pai groaned. He was mortified that Wangtao hadn't pledged he was the only one. And now he couldn't fight his curiosity. "And the youth before me. How long was he with you?"

"Alas, only one full turning of the seasons," Wangtao had said with a low growl. "But enough. I want you to practice coming together." And with that, Wangtao had fisted Pai's yang chu and started to pump it as hard as he could while diving deep inside the youth with his yang chu. And Pai was forced to abandon his questioning at that point and concentrate on coming together as commanded.

And Pai had forgotten what had been said . . . until now. It was already late autumn. Only the winter to go. He could not live without Wangtao. There was nothing in life without Wangtao. He certainly could not go back to Zigui after having lived near Danyang on Tai Hu Lake.

The next market day he did not forget the chi'en, but he came right back to the nanleshijia after he had walked away from it, already knowing the truth, but wanting to be proved wrong.

But he wasn't proved wrong. The other youth was there now, standing on the dock with a beaming Wangtao. Wearing a newly tailored robe from the beautiful scarlet brocade Pai had seen the previous market day. The handsome youth was turning this way and that way, and Wangtao was looking at him with approval—and, yes, Pai was convinced, with that look of speculation and desire that he had seen in Wangtao's eyes when they had first met in Zigui in what seemed so long ago and so far away.

* * * *

Pai stood at the highest point of the Bridge of Sighs between the Tai Hu and Meihung lakes on that first day of winter, still cool but with that touch of frost on the air promising the bleakness to come. He was staring down into the frigid lake water, holding his torn red brocade robe tightly around him, whispering not only of what had gloriously been but, in melancholy, also of what might have been—what he had dreamed would be.

He was not angry—just regretful. If he had stayed in Zigui, life certainly would not have been any better. He had had his peach spring, perfectly ripe summer, and mellow autumn. He would not stand in the way of Wangtao. He had been a superb lover, and Pai loved him still. He would love Wangtao forever.

Pai looked down into the swirling water as it moved from the larger lake into the smaller one, the new water brushing the old water aside, pushing its way into the smaller lake. Life was ever thus. Pai leaned out farther over the stone railing, bending down toward the swirling, welcoming waters.

* * * *

"Pai, Pai," Wangtao was crying out over the water in the advancing twilight as he poled the pleasure barge out onto the large Tai Hu Lake. "Anyone seen my Pai?" he cried out to the other pleasure barges casting off with their first cushioned nesting of treasured clients for the evening.

"Shih, Wangtao *hsien sheng*," another poleman called out to his friend. "Just moments ago, over at the Bridge of Sighs."

"*Hsieh, hsieh*—thanks," Wangtao called back. "It's not like him not to be ready for the first castoff. And I wanted to show him what I had made for him."

"Gifts for a lover?" the friend bantered back, needling him gently. "I've heard you have an ever-stiff yang chu for that one. You know it isn't good business to fall for your cut sleeve."

"Fuck you," Wangtao called back, but in a tone that obviously was given in good humor. "This one is special. I am getting too old for this business. This one I take away with me. And look, see what I had made for him. His robe is old and torn; I've bought him this splendid new scarlet brocade robe. Cost me a month's taking. But he is worth that and more to me. He is worth everything to me."

As they had bantered back and forth, they had been poling across the lake toward the Bridge of Sighs. And as Wangtao had carefully, lovingly folded his love gift and set it down on the cushions at the center of the pleasure barge, he looked across to the entry of the greater Tai Hu Lake into the lesser . . .

. . . and saw the familiar torn red brocade robe floating on the surface of the frigid Tai Hu Lake just below the Bridge of Sighs.

Shun sensed what had happened even before he looked down on Tai Hu Lake from the nanleshijia pavilion deck. He had heard the weeping of the man wafting on the breeze across the lake and had known that it was Wangtao. He stood and looked down upon the boat floating up to the dock, with Wangtao standing and embracing a dripping-wet bundle of red brocade to his chest.

Even having known where the story of Pai and Wangtao would end, Shun was overcome with sadness and turned and walked with weary steps to the strongbox in his room to contemplate whether it was time to flee from this cursed Kingdom of Chu.

Chapter Nine: Xiu and the Jin Devil Captain

Xiu didn't believe the zhaoguzhe, the caretaker of the Cut Sleeve Nanleshijia—men's pleasure house—in Nantung, and he was confused by what the zhaoguzhe was telling him. Since the winter the zhaoguzhe had been suffering under a constant cough, and he had become quite sour. Xiu thought that the old man must be teasing him. He had been training for the bitten peach culmination in the clouds and rain act and was to be auctioned off to the highest bidder at the spring festival, as was Bolin. Xiu's training and preparation had been exacting, and he had already pleasured with the kiss of the yang chu act most of the important and famous men who would be bidding at the seed sowing ceremony to bite his peach and take him into his first clouds and rain. But all contact with these *jen*—men—had been under the watchful eyes of the zhaoguzhe of the Cut Sleeve Nanleshijia in Nantung to ensure that he remained pure of the clouds and rain and did not lose his chenchieh, his chastity, until the ceremony. The zhaoguzhe had said Xiu had done admirably well since he had nearly given himself to the former baoan—house protector—several seasons before.

Xiu had learned well the wiles and enticements that had been taught him to please a patron without blemishing the peach, and the bidding and the bidders themselves were in a frenzy of anticipation.

But one night, weeks before the spring festival, the zhaoguzhe said Xiu's time had come early—and that of Bolin as well—and Xiu and Bolin were roused before dawn the next day and bathed and shaved clean of everything but a silken skein of pigtailed hair at the back of their heads. They also were perfumed, powdered with the enticement powder, and—when what Xiu thought was just one of the zhaoguzhe's cruel training exercises and teases turned to the horror of possibility—shown that they would be clothed in brocaded hanfu—robes—shimmering red for Xiu and deep blue for Bolin—that were being saved for their clouds and rains ceremonies.

That was when the zhaoguzhe told Xiu of the *kueilo*, the foreign ghosts, who were reported to be fierce sailing warriors from the far north and who had appeared off the mouth of the Yangtze River inside a monstrous *chu'an*—vessel—floating beneath a billowing cloud. At first, the zhaoguzhe had said, it was believed that this was the vessel of the pirate Ming Lei, who had been worrying coastal shipping in the region, but that it was since said to be that of tall, large, and rough men from the north—from the land of Jin.

At first Xiu didn't believe him or understand what this had to do with him or Bolin.

"This is far greater than the spring festival, Xiu," the zhaoguzhe had said. "This spreads the renown of Nantung and the Cut Sleeve Nanleshijia all the way to the feet of the Emperor of Jin."

Xiu said that he neither knew nor cared about this faraway land or its ruler, but the zhaoguzhe slapped him for his pouting insolence and continued.

"The Lord of Shi has been put into a quandary, and he has come to me for a solution. This is an opportunity of generations. And you could not be more honored if your chenchieh could be renewed every spring for the highest bidder. In fact, with the favoring of the Lord of Shi, the bidding on you should go up now, even when you no longer are virginal, although I will have to do some fast training and preparation of another for the spring festival. Of course, if you become insolent with me, I could just give you to the Lord of Shi."

Xiu shuddered at the thought of being given to the ruler of the prefecture, the Lord of Shi, as he was reputed to be a very cruel and demanding sexual predator. But when he opened his newly rouged lips to speak, the zhaoguzhe saw the expression on his face and slapped him again, sending clouds of white powder into the air and a flurry of house servants scurrying about to repair the damage to their hours of work on Xiu's face. As luck had it, Xiu still was naked in the wake of the powdering. He would have had better luck if he already had been wound into his red brocade hanfu. The old zhaoguzhe would not have dared ruin those with the spray of white powder. As it was, he was wasting a fortune. The intoxicating, yang chu-hardening powder was a dear commodity.

"I have received overtures from the Jin men on the vessel that they have heard of the house and wish to taste the delights we have here. There was, of course, a veiled threat that if we didn't entertain them with our best, they would burn the nanleshijia. When I reported this to the Lord of Shi and he, in turn, reported it to the King of Wu in Gusu, the king suggested that we entangle the intruders from Jin until he can decide what they are seeking by sailing this far south. I was directed to provide my best jinan to the kueilo. You and Bolin are my best morsels. The king has hinted that if you are successful, you may be bought at a high price for the nanleshijia of the court in Gusu. If you are not successful, I may turn you out into the streets of Nantung, where the fishermen of the town will know what to do with you."

Xiu remained unimpressed. He often had been threatened with the randy fisherman of the town below the cliff on which the men's pleasure house pavilions were perched. And Xiu thought the contact with the King of Wu sounded like fantasy. The house had invested too much in Xiu and Bolin, Xiu thought, for this to be a real threat. At the worst, he would be sold to some dried-up ancient with no seed, flatulence, and a limp yang chu—and that was likely to happen in the spring ceremony anyway.

"We are to provide delay," the zhaoguzhe stubbornly reiterated to Xiu. "You and Bolin are to make the kueilo who appear for you to dally as long as possible. The Lord of Shi does not know if the vessel is a *shangchu'an* or a *chunch'an*, a merchant ship or a war ship. There have been rumors of these kueilo appearing at the fringes of the Central Kingdom, but never here. In either case, they must be made to turn away or go down to the depths of the sea. The Lord of Shi has sent queries to the King of Wu, but the situation is momentous; he must know as soon as the king decides if he can simply kill them or not."

Xiu adopted his humblest look and kowtowed at the zhaoguzhe's feet, searching for the seam where the zhaoguzhe's teasing would collapse. "But I don't understand, caretaker. Why are they coming here to Nantung? We are simply the pleasure resort for the prefecture of Yangzhou. What do we have to do with such momentous affairs?"

The zhaoguzhe patiently tried to explain, which began to make Xiu worry. He didn't usually sustain his teasing this long—or back it up with an expensive costuming. Such reasonableness was not in keeping with the zhaoguzhe's nature. "Panicked for delaying tactics, the emissary to the monster vessel from the Lord of Shi saw the eyes of the kueilo's ch'uanchu, ship's captain, light up at the offer of a respite of clouds and rain at the Cut Sleeve Nanleshijia. When the kueilo captain said he was not interested in a bitten peach—a used jinan—the emissary, knowing of the bidding war on you and Bolin for the spring seed sowing ceremony, spoke of the purity and ripeness of you two. The kueilo captain was said to have become so interested that the interest showed on his body and the emissary was half afraid he himself would be seeded on the spot."

Still Xiu did not believe the zhaoguzhe. Still he thought this was some sort of conditioning joke he was enduring. That it was all part of the ritual. What did the outer world have to do with their small pleasure house high on the cliffs over the bend in the Yangtze River?

But later that afternoon, as Xiu reclined on pillows on the veranda of the Vermilion Pavilion overlooking the sea, trying his best not to transfer any of the enticement powder to the red brocade of his ceremonial robes, he began to believe. He could not believe what he was seeing at first. A giant sea bird slowly appeared from around the eastern point of rocks and glided toward the harbor of the town of Nantung, guided in by a red barge of the Lord of Shi that Xiu recognized from the lord's earlier visits to the Cut Sleeve Nanleshijia. A towering, black-wood vessel driven by billowing clouds of white gossamer.

Xiu shuddered at the thoughts of the visits to the nanleshijia by the Lord of Shi, and of the screams of his jinan brothers behind closed doors during his visits, and of some of them being so ruined they had no longer been able to serve the house. The zhaoguzhe had always tried to hide the jinan in training who would be most profitable for the house when their bite of the peach came, but he wasn't always able to fool the lord. Xiu certainly remembered how distressed the one he had loved, Niu, the house's former baoan, had been when he had stopped here during his own escape from service to the lord. And Xiaodan, sweet little Xiaodan, who had been taken away to the lord's castle and never heard from again.

Bolin was by Xiu's side, in robes of darkest sapphire blue. He shrank from the sight of the giant, floating bird and began to breathe heavily. But Xiu, the more adventuresome of the two, was mesmerized by the sight. And aroused. Xiu had always been scolded for his fantasies and attraction to danger, but these were the same traits that had won him the premier position here, at the pinnacle of empowerment for a jinan. There was no more luxurious life or power over powerful men than the life of a clouds and rain master.

As Bolin's nervousness grew with the far-off vision of inhumanly large figures in strange, black, close-fitting clothing roping down into the Cut Sleeve Nanleshijia launch that had been sent out to their vessel to fetch them, Xiu's interest and curiosity grew.

He now had to believe that the zhaoguzhe had not been teasing him.

For what seemed to be hours but was only a short time, the two could hear the kueilo being ceremoniously welcomed in the reception rooms below them. They heard the wheedling, smooth tones of the zhaoguzhe, covered by a raucous cacophony of hard, guttural sounds from the kueilo. It was obvious that neither understood the other, but as the voices of the foreign ghosts grew louder and their speech slurred, Xiu and Bolin understood that the zhaoguzhe had managed to place them under the spell of the house's special wine, spiced to loosen nerves and cares and enervate the yang chu.

And then two of them were there in the entrance to the Vermilion Pavilion, one on each side of the zhaoguzhe, and with a semicircle of slack-jawed and murmuring tunic-clad house servants behind them.

They were both monstrous. The taller of the two, quite evidently the *ch'uanchu*—ship's captain, was a *hungmao*—a red-haired devil. Xiu had read of such in the classics, but these two were monsters from beyond the pale. The obvious leader of the two, the ship's captain, stood there, a full head taller than the zhaoguzhe. And such a head it was. Fully encircled with bright red, curly hair—on top and down the sides and under his chin and his nose. Broad shouldered and thin waisted, he was swathed in a clinging sweat-soaked, rough tunic and leggings and heavy fur-lined boots, which were not just exotic, but they also must be stifling in the heat of the nanleshijia's subtropical province. Xiu could smell him from where he stood, a pace in front of the trembling Bolin. A meat eater. Underneath the hair and clothing, Xiu could see that the man was of palest hue, the source of the name that had been given to these recent interlopers on the world of the Central Kingdom—*the* world. That name was "ghost."

The other man, not much taller than the zhaoguzhe, but much thicker, all hard muscle, in the body and similarly clothed to the other kueilo, stood beside and slightly back from the hungmao, another signal of who was the most important. This second foreign ghost had hair of the tawniest gold, not an auspicious color. Legends had reached the village of Nantung of other such golden-haired spear and shield-brandishing men visiting from the outside, across the deserts to the west, naked but for short skirts around their middles and sandals on their feet in times past. But all of the stories of them said that they had been famous for their cruelty and that they had been absorbed and destroyed as they deserved. This second kueilo standing before them, one step back from his ch'uanchu, exuded this sense of cruelty. He had a gold ring in one ear and a black patch over one eye, and a leering stare that bore right through Xiu and Bolin.

Bolin shrank behind Xiu, but Xiu looked up—indeed they were built so tall and broad that one had to look up—at the kueilo with disdain and with a haughtiness that Xiu had been taught drove some men wild with wanting. Xiu felt all tingly, ready for the challenge that the zhaoguzhe had claimed that the King of Wu had set for him—and that Xiu was more than half way to believing now that the strange, overpowering kueilo had been produced.

But the men smelled to high heaven. Before Xiu could stomach even pleasuring either one of them in a kiss of the yang chu act, he declared haughtily, they would have to be cleaned. And Xiu told the zhaoguzhe so in no uncertain terms. His eyes flashed, but he realized, Xiu was sure, that there were limits to what either Xiu or Bolin could do with an unwashed meat eater. Besides, as Xiu was soon to find out, the zhaoguzhe had already anticipated that need.

As soon as Xiu spoke, the eyes of both kueilo focused on him and both smiled that smile he had already seen a hundred times at the Cut Sleeve Nanleshijia. They both wanted him. But it was the exotic pale blue eyes of the hungmao ch'uanchu that Xiu met with his, and both knew in an instant the pairings were settled.

If Xiu had known beforehand what would happen then, he would have acted differently. But the future, even the immediate future, was not for solitary *Chungkuojen*—Chinese man—like Xiu to know—this was knowledge reserved to the King of Wu or at least one no lower in the order than the Lord of Shi.

The zhaoguzhe motioned for Xiu and Bolin to rise and part. Xiu was waved toward the eastern chamber off the Vermilion Pavilion and Bolin toward the western chamber. The zhaoguzhe nudged the hungmao toward the east and the golden-haired kueilo toward the west, which they both immediately acknowledged and acceded to. The house servants split behind the zhaoguzhe, one half gliding toward the eastern chamber and the other half toward the western chamber.

Xiu heard Bolin mutter a cut-off exclamation as he and the golden-haired kueilo both reached the entrance to the western chamber. This was unheard of—for a clouds and rain master to say anything at this stage of the act—and Xiu's head snapped around at the sound. The golden-haired kueilo had already laid hands on Bolin. When Bolin involuntarily shrank away from him, the golden-haired kueilo backhanded him across the cheek with such a mighty blow that Bolin was propelled through the entrance of the western chamber. The golden-haired kueilo turned and gave the house servants moving in his direction a menacing look that stopped them dead in their tracks, and they retreated, backing away from him and bowing low at the waist.

Xiu's eyes went to the zhaoguzhe for reaction. Under normal circumstances, he would have used his martial arts skills to neutralize such a crass and out-of-control patron. But, though Xiu could see that zhaoguzhe's jaw was set and his body tensed on the edge, he did nothing. The zhaoguzhe looked stricken and he held a hand to his chest like he was in pain. The look he gave to Xiu conveyed that there was nothing he could do—that what was unfolding here was being played on a larger stage than their nanleshijia. That's when Xiu knew without a doubt that this was a reality. That all the zhaoguzhe had said about the directive from the King of Wu and the importance of delaying the kueilos' return to the Kingdom of Jin was true. True and necessary. Important. Perhaps vital to maintaining civilization as the mere pawns in the Cut Sleeve Nanleshijia knew it.

The sounds from the western chamber were rending. The tearing of cloth—which Xiu could see was tearing equally at the emotions of the zhaoguzhe, something Xiu could well understand, knowing the price of a spring ceremonial robe—the crude gruntings of the kueilo in immediate and full rut, and the cries of Bolin, cries that were unthinkable in the Cut Sleeve Nanleshijia—except perhaps when the Lord of Shi visited. But the bones the lord was tossed were of much less valuable flesh than either Xiu or Bolin. To sacrifice the virginity of such as Xiu and Bolin was unprecedented.

Xiu and the zhaoguzhe stood there, looking at each other and then at the hungmao—the captain of the Jin vessel—standing between them and giving them a sneer of a smile and winks. They knew in no uncertain terms that the clouds and rain had already started in the western chamber and that Bolin's chenchieh—his chastity—was as good as undone. Xiu knew that any delay was now entirely his to provide, although the looks the hungmao gave him and the hands he was placing on Xiu's curves within his ceremonial robe brought doubt into Xiu's mind on what he alone could do.

At the doorway to the eastern chamber, Xiu turned and looked up into the pale blue eyes of the hungmao and tried to convey with every fiber of his being that foreign monster would have him but not in the way and at the pace that the golden-haired kueilo was having Bolin. He seemed to understand, and Xiu was heartened to get the impression that he took his pleasures—and gave the client his pleasure—at a much more easy pace than his compatriot did.

At the interior end of the eastern chamber was a bathing tub with steaming water in it. At the open end of the pavilion, overlooking the curve in the Yangtze River, was a pallet of red silk with mountains of red silk pillow cushions, the home of the clouds and rain, where Xiu was now resigned that he would become a bitten peach—that he was about to lose his chenchieh.

The hungmao stood in the center of the room, an amused look on his face, and his arms outstretched and legs in a wide stance, as the house servants slowly but methodically figured out how to unclothe him. The zhaoguzhe stood in the doorway from the Vermilion Pavilion, watching the hungmao being disrobed. Even though he was trembling from some infirmity, he would stand there and observe until the completion of the first clouds and rain. It was his duty to do so—to observe and record the time and place of Xiu's loss of the chenchieh that the Cut Sleeve Nanleshijia prized so highly. It would be marked in vermilion ink, the highest honor—at the pleasure of the Lord of Shi. Even higher than a link to the spring festival seed sowing ceremony would have been. It added stacks of *hsienchien*, cash, to Xiu's worth for each subsequent clouds and rain assignation.

The visiting Jin kueilo monsters would become the talk of the kingdom—especially when rumors of their yang chu equipment—which Bolin now knew intimately and Xiu was about to—began to float around. Clients would flock to the Cut Sleeve Nanleshijia to thrill in being where the giants from beyond the kingdom had been with their tree-trunk yang chu. "Aeiii," the clients would be heard to say. "I felt I could walk upright in the channel that kueilo drilled."

The zhaoguzhe obviously could not observe the moment for Bolin, which, from the sounds from the other chamber had already taken place and was moving into a second taking, but the zhaoguzhe was a modern jen of practicality. He would simply record what he hadn't actually seen, and he knew that Xiu would not naysay him, even though it was his duty to do so; he knew that Xiu would not subject Bolin to that dishonor and loss of future status.

Xiu's eyes were also on those of the hungmao. His eyes were focused on the peach he was about to bite. He wanted to see Xiu's reaction to his nakedness. And, trained as Xiu was, he was already prepared to respond with embarrassment and awe. Xiu had been trained to do this for a eunuch or castrati, if faced with that in this situation and they had been given access to him by the zhaoguzhe. Xiu needed no training to fall back on, though. The hungmao was huge in ways Xiu had never seen in life before. There was a statue the height of three men in the entrance hall to the nanleshijia with an erect phallus to assure clients they were in a nanleshijia—and the jinan often joked about fucking themselves on this triple-sized appendage. But Xiu gasped without feigning now to see a yang chu in real life that rivaled it.

The hungmao's body was well formed and hard and bulging in muscles, obviously from hard, honest work. He was covered in red, curly hair everywhere. And his yang chu was alarmingly heavy and long and thick. Xiu gulped and his eyes went wide open and his jaw slack—all movements he had been trained in to please the jen he would be given to, but movements that came naturally under these circumstances. Xiu's channel tightened at the thought that for the first time he would be doing more to entertain a client's yang chu than fondling it and mouthing it—and that he would have to do it with what was standing up from the hungmao's belly. Xiu involuntarily moaned. His reaction pleased the hungmao, which Xiu could readily see as the giant's yang chu rose up parallel with the matting on the floor and filled out impossibly larger.

The hungmao went into the bath with the help of the house servants. A couple of these carried off his clothing, undoubtedly to be double boiled, and the other house servants began scrubbing him in earnest. The past year's spring festival clouds and rain master, Wangan, glided into the room with willowy stride and, after slowly shrugging out of all but his diaphanous inner robe, knelt beside the tub. His hands went into the soapy water, and Xiu watched the hungmao's eyes slit and the pleasure fan out across his face as Wangan enclosed his hands around the hungmao's yang chu and began to stroke.

It was Xiu's time then—the beginning of the ceremony of the clouds and rain. He stood there, between the tub and the sea, between the hungmao and the pallet of his chenchieh farewell and untied the sash on his layers of hanfu and began to slowly unwind his red ceremonial robe and the deep purple under robe. Xiu took a long time doing this, and the hungmao's eyes were glued to his form the entire time. From where he stood Xiu could hear the giant sighing from where he stood from the ministrations of Wangan's delicate, expert hands and fingers on the kueilo's yang chu. Almost as if not realizing what he was doing, the hungmao had one hand searching inside the folds of Wangan's robes, where he obviously found what he was looking for and was stroking it. His other hand was lifted above his head and had snaked into

132

the tunic of one of the house servants scrubbing at him and had exposed and was tweaking a nipple.

After a slow, orchestrated, long-practiced performance of revealing himself, Xiu stood there before him, the folds of the red and purple robes swirling around his feet. Xiu placed his hands on his hips and swayed ever so imperceptively from side to side. Xiu was not more than half the hungmao's size. Lithe and willowy, but muscle hard from years of ever-higher-level tai chi practice. Naked and completely shaved. His were the pert little yang chu and ball sac that Chungkuojen so highly prized in their clouds and rain masters. Xiu worried briefly if this would please a kueilo as well, but the look he cast on the ripe peach's revealed body left no doubt that he did. As was wanted in a spring festival master, Xiu had the years of an adult but the body of a youth.

The hungmao gave Xiu a wicked smiled. He reached up and pulled a surprised Wangan into the tub with him and turned the now sputtering jinan onto his belly, with his arms over the side of the tub and his nipples, freed now from the transparent, soaked robe by the hungmao's rough hands, resting on the lip of the tub. His eyes were wildly racing around the inside of the pavilion, trying to focus on something that would help him understand why he was in this position and where his saving help could come from. Did this kueilo have no sense whatsoever for the ceremonies of the clouds and rain?

The hungmao, crouching over the submerged hips of the jinan, never let his own gaze free that of Xiu, who stood there, frozen amid his symbolic blood-red pillows and pallet covering, trembling and trying not to show his fear and consternation, as Wangan let out a cry of violation and skewering as he never had experienced before. Xiu understood perfectly that this was a matter of foreplay between the hungmao and himself. The groaning and moaning that Wangan's gaping mouth was producing and his wild-eyed looks of impossibly full and cruel possession—and even the roiling of the tub water signaling the power and rapidity of the hungmao's thrusts—were all to demonstrate how the hungmao intended to possess and overpower Xiu himself.

The message was not lost on Xiu, and inside he was all turmoil mixed with anticipation, while on the outside he fought to maintain a haughty continence free from intimidation.

This was all just preliminary posturing by the kueilo, however. He was doing nothing but increasing his arousal and the length and thickness of his yang chu. He quickly lost all interest in Wangan and the house servant and, indeed, in his bath, although, happily he had been scrubbed sufficiently already. He rose up out of the tub, leaving the servants to help a whimpering Wangan rise and stumble out of the pavilion. The bit of appetizer the hungmao had indulged in and the effect of Xiu's own disrobing had caused the hungmao's yang chu to rise and fill out to put to shame the most virile of the stud horses in the Cut Sleeve Nanleshijia—the young men kept well away from the pavilions Xiu and Bolin lived in, the big-cocked young men who some clients came to visit for their own enhanced clouds and rain entertainments.

Xiu moved breathlessly to the hungmao, kneeling before him and gently enclosing the base of the giant's yang chu in his small fists, one above the other, and still leaving more than Xiu thought his mouth could accommodate. In a rustle of naked feet and soft silk, Xiu sensed more than heard the last of the house servants evaporate beyond the bamboo screens.

For the next several minutes, as the hungmao sighed and growled, rocked back and forth on the pads of his gigantic feet, and breathed heavily and noisily, he moved Xiu's head between his enormous paws while the jinan entertained him with everything he had learned in the art of the kiss and suck of the yang chu.

The hungmao was getting bigger and bigger and was pumping ever more rapidly with his yang chu inside the young jinan's mouth. Xiu's hands went to the giant's heavy orbs. Xiu could hardly enclose them in his hands, they were so large and tightly balled. None that Xiu had handled before now were anything like this size. The kueilo was a monster of a man, and Xiu was wondering if he was typical of his people of the north, beyond civilization, or a monster among them as well, as Xiu felt his bulbous knob pressing against the back of his throat.

Xiu lightly squeezed on the orbs, wanting him to drain himself now, before the clouds and rain, to delay that. Every moment of delay was precious time. Xiu understood that now.

But, with a roar, the hungmao, pulled the small jinan up and off his throbbing yang chu. He turned his prey and pushed him down on all fours, and Xiu understood that he was going to be invaded and become a bitten peach right there and then, years of training and preparation erased in one thrust of the sword.

That could not be, though. The customs and rules of a kingdom of Wu nanleshijia were quite explicit. Xiu had to lose his chenchieh on the red pallet across the chamber. The zhaoguzhe quietly grunted from across the room, where he was watching and assessing the taking, obviously making the same point. If the protocol wasn't followed, Xiu's future worth as a courtesan jinan would be jeopardized. But Xiu didn't need the zhaoguzhe to remind him of the ceremony requirements. Xiu had been studying these ceremonial requirements for four season cycles.

Xiu disengaged from the hungmao somehow and half crawled and half scuttled toward the red pallet. The hungmao misinterpreted, assuming most probably, that he had frightened Xiu too much and that the jinan was trying to escape. The renewed cries from the other chamber across the Vermilion Pavilion only added credence to this thought. Bolin was being plowed hard and rough, as he was loudly and plaintively complaining of—just like a stable boy, completely wiping away his dignity and social status. Xiu could only hope that only the zhaoguzhe and he remained to hear of his dishonoring—that the house servants were well beyond hearing. But Xiu knew that was a hopeless thought. All that comforted Xiu was knowing that any house servant heard gossiping about this night would lose his tongue—and maybe his yang chu as well—and that the servant would just need to be paid under the table to affirm that all of the ceremonial requirements were met.

Xiu's perceived attempt to escape didn't cool the giant sea captain down. It only increased his ardor. This is how he liked to take his captives in sea battles—the panicked young men scuttling ineffectually across the boards of his ship's deck. No place to go. Their cries of anguish when he caught up with them and rode their bodies down to the decking. The piercing scream of his victory as he thrust inside their channels.

The hungmao reached Xiu and toppled him down on his belly in a cloud of white powder as the jinan reached the red silk pallet. Xiu did manage, however, to pull up onto the pallet on his hands and knees as the hungmao encased his hips between his strong knees. Technically, the customs were being satisfied—if only barely, as any client with the money to pay to bite the peach for the first time was refined enough to do so in full accordance with the proper rituals, which did not include brutality and wild taking. If wild taking was what the client wanted, he had to return another time as a patron.

Xiu heard the rustle of the zhaoguzhe's robes as he decorously approached with a pot of scented clouds and rain ointment and calmed the hungmao long enough to convey that he was trying to aid the inevitable act. The hungmao held Xiu down on all fours with one arm wrapped around his chest as he crouched over the jinan and invaded his tight and virginal anus with lubricated fingers. At the same time, the zhaoguzhe worked ointment on the hungmao's prodigious, throbbing yang chu.

Xiu had the sense then of being in the embrace of a silken-pelted bear as the zhaoguzhe faded back to the entrance of the chamber and the hungmao held the bulbous head of his yang chu to the jinan's back entrance in an encasing, directing fist.

The hungmao panted hard as he worked himself inside Xiu, and the now-bitten peach panted even harder and suppressed his groans and moans as best he could as the giant did so. The groaning and moaning was meant to be saved for later, when the patron was fully saddled and was stroking and needed to hear that he was the master of the Central Kingdom.

But Xiu could not help it. He cried out in pain and invasion, nothing like this having been part of what he had learned over the last four season cycles. Although, to rights, no one involved in his training could have been known that he was destined to lose his chenchieh to a monster horse-sized foreign ghost yang chu.

"I must not faint," Xiu kept repeating to himself. "I must pleasure him with my body for as long as possible." Xiu gritted his teeth and took the monster cock inside his channel and clenched his entrance muscles as he had been taught and listened in triumph to the hungmao gasp in pleasure at that. And then, as the monster yang chu sank in and in and in, Xiu tried, through the wall of pain, to conjure up all of the exercises he had learned to control the muscles inside him. To make them ripple around and across the kueilo's yang chu, to make internal love to his manhood as he had been taught to do. The clouds, the important clouds before the rain—the beating of one cloud against the other, the friction that brought on the rain, with the greater the cloud beating, the greater the rain.

The kueilo groaned and gasped in pleasure and his lips went to the hollow of Xiu's neck, where they ingested the enticement powder. He murmured and sighed and moaned, and Xiu felt the powder working in the impossible reality that the throbbing yang chu grew even larger inside the compromised channel. His horse yang chu slid back and forth, shallow and then deep, to the surface and then diving down, down, down and holding as Xiu's muscles contracted around him and worked on his yang chu.

Xiu could hear Bolin screaming out that he was being split asunder and that his insides were being flooded—again— from the other chamber, and Xiu began to wiggle his hips, no longer in as much pain as at the beginning. Something else was moving inside him now. Wanting. Actually wanting this clouds and rain. He was working the clouds—the touching and the sighing and the moaning and the movement under him and back against him as he thrust, meeting the giant thrust for thrust now. Listening to his ragged breathing. Giving him the best clouds he had ever received. Living up to the reputation of the Cut Sleeve Nanleshijia.

Then the rains came. The hungmao cried out in ecstasy and the rains came. Deep inside Xiu's channel. One, two, three gushings. The kueilo collapsed on top of Xiu, pushing him down on his belly on the red silk pallet, and Xiu heard the rustling of the zhaoguzhe's robes as he left the pavilion, his official duties finished—back to his dark room and his vermilion ink and his triumphant collection of a favor from the Lord of Shi, a favor that could sustain the Cut Sleeve Nanleshijia for generations to come.

As the zhaoguzhe wrote out his report, he took time to write it in flowery language and giving the swallowing of the peach its full, detailed description. He wasn't just writing for the record. This story would be floated throughout the prefecture. The men's house of pleasure would not lose in Xiu's inability to qualify for the spring clouds and rain auction. The story of the thunderstorm with the giant foreign devil and the tree trunk of a yang chu Xiu's channel had satisfied would disseminate like wild fire, and rich patrons would flock to the nanleshijia to follow the pathway the hungmao had reamed. As he wrote, the sharp ache in his chest settled on zhaoguzhe. He did not feel that he had much time left, but he should have enough to pen this legend to parchment with the traditional vermillion ink.

Xiu heard Bolin crying out from the other chamber. He was screaming that his wrists had been tied and he was doubled over the rim of the unused tub and was being roughly entered again and again and again. That the golden-haired kueilo smelled vile and cruelly bit and had a yang chu thicker than the pillars in the Vermilion Pavilion. That his rains were a flood. But there was nothing Xiu could do for Bolin now. Bolin had abandoned all sense of decorum and the best that anyone could do for him now was to forget what they had heard from him.

Xiu had to delay the departure of the vessel. And he knew it would not leave without its captain. Perhaps if he could detain him even for a night.

That was, of course, not permitted in the clouds and rain ceremony. Once the peach had been bitten, the ceremony was over. The jinan was to retire to his nanleshijia and engage in ritual cleansing ceremonies that could take up to a full phase of the moon. In the interim, unless the man who had bitten the peach wanted to pay to step forward as sole patron, the zhaoguzhe started to set up subscriptions for the new jinan's services. After the cleansing period, the jinan was available to entertain all who wanted him and could pay for him in succession as long as he could maintain interest or his body could endure the entertainment.

But that initial clouds and rain? Just the one ritual.

The hungmao rolled off Xiu and lay on his back on the platform, still panting. Gathering all of the resolve and resources he could, Xiu sat up and moved his head over the hungmao's heaving chest and started to lick his nipples and set his red chest hair aswirl. Xiu's hands danced over his torso and down to his yang chu, still huge but now in repose. Despite tradition, Xiu knew he needed to coax him into clouds and rain again. Xiu needed him to believe that only with this lover could he accomplish rapid recovery and multiple clouds and rain. Wanting to stay with Xiu as long as possible. Xiu knew this was vital to the pride of any man, Chungkuojen or kueilo. All the same in the vanity realm. Entice three clouds and rain in an assignation, and the man is yours forever.

Xiu put an arm around the hungmao's neck and lifted his mouth to his nipple. The kueilo sucked and licked Xiu's nub while Xiu worked his other hand across his cheek. Xiu moved the hungmao's mouth around the nipple, coaxing him to ingest more of the enticement powder, which he did. This had the desired effect, in consort with the jinan's stroking, on his yang chu. The giant was regaining virility. Xiu stroked the slit in the head of his yang chu with the tip of his finger, and the kueilo gasped and began to writhe in pleasure, his life's fluid beginning to bubble up onto Xiu's finger. The jinan felt him trembling at the knowledge that there would be a second clouds and rain so soon after the first. He already was nearly a captive of the bitten peach.

After Xiu heard the last gurgling cry from Bolin from across the Vermilion Pavilion, followed by an ominous silence, Bolin's friend felt more than saw the presence of the golden-haired kueilo at the entrance to the eastern chamber. His ragged breathing could be clearly heard. Xiu knew he was watching the hungmao and Xiu deeply entering their second clouds and rain.

The hungmao was kneeling, sitting back on his calves and facing out toward the sunset over the bend in the Yangtze. He was holding his new conquest, like a small doll, in front of him, Xiu facing the river as well, his knees leveraging off the surface of the red-silk pallet, body arched out, and his anus sliding up and down on the hungmao's rejuvenated yang chu. Up and down, endlessly. Xiu no longer was in pain. He was enjoying the taking. He wondered if he would ever be swallowing a member this large again. Stretching for it. Perfecting the skills of internal muscle massage of a throbbing horse yang chu of impossible size and strength.

The hungmao was sighing and groaning contentedly.

A shadow fell on Xiu, and he no longer could see the river. What he saw now was a short, thick yang chu jutting out of a thick thatch of golden hair. Xiu almost gagged at the thickness and smelliness of the second kueilo's yang chu as it was pushed between his lips. But this was no time for niceties. Xiu gave the golden hair a quite satisfactory kiss of the yang chu too. He was determined to keep the two here as long as possible. If Bolin had failed, Xiu could only try to succeed.

The golden-haired kueilo grabbed Xiu's pigtail, forced his head back, and pushed hard down inside his mouth with his yang chu. The hungmao, between pants of his own spoke sharply at the golden one in that ugly guttural language of theirs, though, and the golden-haired kueilo released Xiu's pigtail.

The virile hungmao was still sliding Xiu up and down on his yang chu when the golden one released his seed inside Xiu's mouth. He brought his mouth down to Xiu's and sucked his fluid from inside the jinan's mouth in a lips-on-lips invasion that was almost never performed between men at the Cut Sleeve Nanleshijia. But if it delayed their parting for even a moment, Xiu was determined to do it. Xiu returned his kiss and stifled his surprise and pain when the giant bit the jinan on the lip.

The golden one knelt down before Xiu and the jinan felt his fingers forcing their way inside his anus alongside the sliding yang chu of the hungmao. He was stroking his own yang chu back to thickness with his other hand, and for a brief moment Xiu panicked at the sure knowledge that he intended his yang chu to join that of the hungmao's inside his channel.

But the hungmao spoke gruffly to the golden one, and he pulled his fingers from Xiu and stood and moved toward the door. Xiu knew from what he was saying that he was telling the hungmao it was time for them to return to the vessel in the lagoon.

Xiu tightened his internal muscles on the hungmao's yang chu and captured his lips and gave him lip-to-lip attention for the first time in their session of clouds and rain. He reacted with surprise and pleasure, and then Xiu took his head and buried the giant's lips into his shoulder, where there still was some enticement powder lingering. He was lost to Xiu then.

He and the golden-haired kueilo exchanged hurried and angry words. As they spoke, Xiu performed the fan movement of the clouds and rain. In one deft, lithe movement, he turned on the hungmao's yang chu to where Xiu was facing him and, at the same time, pushed him down onto his back, with his muscle-bulging hairy legs now stretched out toward the river.

With the golden-haired kueilo still angrily talking and gesturing and the hungmao groaning loudly in ecstasy and his pale-blue eyes revolving wildly in their sockets, Xiu began to ride his yang chu hard, with revolving hips and rippling internal muscles. The golden one gave up in disgust and departed, while his captain writhed in deep lust under the jinan. The hungmao flooded Xiu's channel with his essence soon thereafter.

The hungmao drifted off to sleep hours later after the third clouds and rain, in which Xiu lay on his back, his hips raised by red silk pillows, his legs flared out wide, and the hungmao on his knees on the red pallet between his legs, looking out at the now-furled sails of his vessel riding quietly in the surface of the river and moving his hips and centering deep, plowing back and forth, rhythmically and forever, while Xiu sighed and moaned for him, letting him know he was the most masterful jen in the Central Kingdom. Holding him enthralled with every trick Xiu had learned.

Xiu performed clouds and rain, each time in a different position and ever more intricately, holding the hungmao's total attention between replenishment meals supplied by a delighted zhaoguzhe, for the next three days and nights.

When the hungmao finally descended to his vessel, stiff legged and humming, on the fourth day, Xiu was at the edge of the veranda of the Vermilion Pavilion, only slightly happy to see him go. He had a yang chu such as Xiu would never again ride, a yang chu that the zhaoguzhe would have expertly measured in length and thickness in his mind and in his handling during the clouds and rain ointment application and would record on the official record of capability. But it wasn't just the size of him that enhanced Xiu's value to the Cut Sleeve Nanleshijia; as Xiu's clouds and rain became more inventive, the hungmao had become more and more gentle and lost to him. If the Lord of Shi had instructed that he be held here forever, Xiu could have managed that—and would have been content doing it.

Xiu could part from him with the knowledge that his fortune and legend was now made, not just in the Cut Sleeve Nanleshijia, but also beyond the pleasure resort of Nantung— perhaps even beyond the entire prefecture of Yangzhou. Xiu could dream of being lionized to the King of Wu himself. Perhaps he could dream of serving the yang chu needs and desires of the Son of Heaven himself.

But as much as Xiu had come to enjoy the hungmao's horse yang chu churning inside him, Xiu remained Chungkuojen to the very fiber of him. He sensed that these kueilo, these foreign ghosts, were devils to be avoided and kept away from the purity of the Central Kingdom. At least he could rest in the knowledge that his four days of delay had given the Lord of Shi the time he needed to devise plans to eradicate this threat—to ensure that no kueilo ghost ships would enter the mouth of the Yangtze River or the bays of any other city in the Central Kingdom ever again.

But these thoughts were quickly lost to Xiu. With the visit of the Jin kueilo, his whole life and environment had changed. When the kueilo was gone, Xiu found out that, although Bolin had survived his cruel clouds and rain experience, it was only barely and perhaps only for the present. Xiu found him on his cot, torn and nearly delirious. He didn't have much time for concern for Bolin as he also had been informed that the zhaoguzhe had been found dead on his office floor shortly after Xiu had accomplished his feat of imprisoning the hungmao in clouds and rain for four days and nights. The call had already gone out to the kingdom for a new zhaoguzhe, as a nanleshijia could not function without one.

The most significant change in Xiu's life, though, was that he no longer was in training to be a jinan; he was a bitten peach. And he was a famous jinan now. In the ensuing weeks, though, nothing in his life became regularized again. He was belatedly being given his full-moon period of rest after his initial clouds and rain, but rich notables far and wide were eager to sign his schedule book.

For now, though, there was no zhaoguzhe at the Cut Sleeve Nanleshijia to give order to the further professional life of the brave Xiu.

Chapter Ten: The Return

It was difficult to tell that they were even engaging in clouds and rain. The rice merchant was perhaps Xiu's most refined client. He was a connoisseur of the tea ceremony, and anyone passing by the chamber would have thought that this was all the merchant Fu Yang and the young jinan —male prostitute—were doing: drinking tea and having an intimate moment.

And having an intimate moment was exactly what they were having. They were kneeling, closely side by side, on a tatami mat in front of a tea service on a low table. They were both clothed in rich-colored silk hanfu—robes—which billowed around their bodies in folds that intertwined with each other. The merchant had an arm around Xiu, holding him closely into his side. Xiu was twisted away from Fu and rolled over on his thigh and hip. Somewhere in the twisted folks of the two men's hanfu an opening had been created that permitted access to Xiu's channel by Fu's yang chu—cock. The rice merchant was slowly and languidly pulling Xiu on and off his yang chu by the pressure and release of his arm around the jinan's body.

Xiu caught the hint of motion at the door to the chamber and looked over to see the new zhaoguzhe—caretaker, manager of the Cut Sleeve men's pleasure house—peeking around the door frame. He signaled to Xiu that they had something to discuss. Xiu inclined his head. He usually didn't rush Fu when he visited, sometimes letting him overstay his time. Xiu was too senior to have to stay within the set bounds on time, and for the men who were the most attentive in scheduling his time, he liked to extend the time, telling them that it was because they were so good to him. That kept them coming back and paying well—and bringing him gifts for himself.

The zhaoguzhe's signal, though, told Xiu to keep the session short. The caretaker would not have interrupted the session if he did not have something important to discuss with Xiu. The new zhaoguzhe was as strict, organized, and commanding as the old one had been. Xiu wondered if all zhaoguzhe were alike. This one had stepped in like he knew the Cut Sleeve Nanleshijia intimately and had a schedule set up for Xiu almost before his month of rest after the initiating clouds and rain ceremony was over. Considering the unusual demands made on Xiu for his first clouds and rain experience, he might have asked for extra rest—he had done so for Bolin, who still had not recovered from the assault of the rough, golden-haired kueilo sailor—but the new zhaoguzhe reviewed the requests coming in for Xiu's services and decided that the benefits to be had of scheduling Xiu within the usual custom was just too tempting to pass up.

Xiu turned his face to Fu's and took the merchant's lips in his. The merchant was surprised—but not angry—at this forwardness by Xiu.

"I'm sorry, sire, I cannot resist you," Xiu murmured. "You are irresistible to me in your attentions. You make me lose control."

The rice merchant grunted his surprise and pleasure as Xiu moved his buttocks up onto Fu's lap without losing the purchase of the merchant's yang chu inside him, and started to pump his pelvis up and down on the cock, moaning and sighing, and congratulating the merchant on the size and strength of his yang chu.

Fu ejaculated well before his usual time was up, but he had been given such a surprising and unusual clouds and rain that he gave no complaint, not even realizing he was being bundled out earlier than usual.

When Xiu came to the zhaoguzhe's office after kissing the rice merchant away, he discovered that the issue was connected with the benefits to the nanleshijia's treasury that the zhaoguzhe could not resist. He found the caretaker talking in hushed and serious tones with his associate, a strange, quiet young man from the north of the kingdom of Wu who the zhaoguzhe had brought with him.

The zhaoguzhe looked up at Xiu as he entered, almost startled that the jinan had been able to end his session so quickly.

"Don't worry," Xiu said. "Fu Yang left happy."

"You are such a blessing to the nanleshijia, Xiu," the zhaoguzhe said. "I am quite sorry what must be done. But there is no choice. You have been requested specifically."

Xiu didn't speak. He was accustomed to not being the one in any scheme that was given notice or preference.

"You have, no doubt, heard of the pirate, Ming Lei?" The zhaoguzhe spoke in a low voice, while looking around the office, as if the walls had ears.

"Yes, certainly. Who has not? What of him? I have heard that he has not been bothering the shipping at the mouth of the Yangtze recently."

"He hasn't because he's been up the river bothering the shipping up there."

"And you know this because—?"

"Because his emissary has told us so."

"His emissary?" Xiu didn't like the thought of where this was heading.

"Yes. Ming Lei is coming here, to the nanleshijia. Under a cover of secrecy, of course."

"And he is coming to clouds and rain with me?"

"Yes. We have no choice, really. There is a threat of raiding us and burning us out if we do not cooperate. The emissary wasn't at all delicate about establishing that."

"And a threat of the same if we inform the prefecture authorities he will be here, as well?"

"No threat was needed, Xiu. If we tell the Lord of Shi the pirate is here, our world will surely end in the ensuing attempt to capture or kill him. All that you have heard of the reputation of the Lord of Shi is true. He is ruthless and wouldn't think twice of burning us out as soon as you were engaged with the pirate captain. This is a time to be quiet and politic. And that is not all I must inform you of."

"What else is there, zhaoguzhe?"

"The reports that the Jin kueilo and their war ship are sailing off the mouth of the Yangtze again are also true. And I know this, as I am sure you are going to ask, because they too have sent an emissary saying the captain wishes your services again. I'm sorry, Xiu."

Xiu was not quite as sorry at the prospect of another clouds and rain experience with the hungmao with the gigantic yang chu as he was with the unknown pirate captain, who was known for ruthless cruelty. But he would not show this to the zhaoguzhe.

"Which will come to me first?" was Xiu's simple question. He was resolved to do what he was trained to do. He just wished that he would not be used as a political pawn.

"The pirate Ming Lei."

"When?"

"Tomorrow, in the dark of night."

"I will be prepared, of course."

* * * *

The zhaoguzhe and his assistant stood by the dock below the cliff-top compound of pavilions making up the Cut Sleeve Nanleshijia for nearly two hours in the dark of the next night. The assistant was holding a lantern, muffled on the land side with a cloth, so that the beacon could only be seen from the waters of the Yangtze. Both men were dressed in black

147

hanfu. They didn't want to call attention to their vigil, and they needed to be the ones to greet the pirate, Ming Lei. Very few at the nanleshijia knew of his planned visit. The fewer who knew the more likely that the Lord of Shi would never know the pirate had visited the nanleshijia. The zhaoguzhe could easily lose his head for not warning the authorities. The pirate had put the nanleshijia in a very tough spot.

As the two looked out to the river, the clouds that had been scuttling across the sky, blotting out the full moon, moved away, and the zhaoguzhe could see the outline of a vessel that must be that of Ming Lei. He also now could hear the muffled oars dipping through the water as a small boat with three figures in it approached the dock.

The boat hit the dock and one of the figures jumped out and tied a rope from the boat to an iron ring in one of the dock's posts. The figure that had been in the middle of the boat—a man of great height and imposing figure—climbed to the dock and approached. The zhaoguzhe's assistant lifted the lantern to shine on the countenance of the late night visitor.

"You!" the pirate and the zhaoguzhe exclaimed in unison, and, with surprise, in a louder tone than either had expected to be speaking, privacy not being a concern of one any more than of the other.

"Niu?" the zhaoguzhe then said, in a more hushed tone.

"Shun?" the pirate promptly countered.

"You are the pirate Ming Lei?" the zhaoguzhe asked in disbelief. "The last I knew you had been taken before the King of Wu."

"That ultimately did not work out too well. So you are the zhaoguzhe of the famous Cut Sleeve Nanleshijia now? I thought you were dead. I was told that the raiding party from the kingdom of Chu had killed you, although no one would show me a body. Several said they saw a killing sword stroke applied to your back."

"I think your dirty tunics in the pack on my back saved me."

Niu laughed. "You must tell me how you came to return to Nantung. And this, your assistant," Niu said, with an indulgent smile, turning his attention to the young man at Shun's side. "Haven't I seen him before too?"

"I trust the story of my journey here is as unusual and blessed with luck as yours. And you should recognize my assistant, Rong, here. But I'm surprised you do. He became a bitten peach under you the night before we parted. But you enjoyed the virginity of so many young men—and threw them aside without another thought or look thereafter. I'm surprised you can distinguish one of them from any of the others." This was spoken almost bitterly. Shun himself had been used thusly many seasons ago, right here in Nantung, when Niu was the baoan—protector—of the Cut Sleeve Nanleshijia and Shun was a mere servant of the establishment.

"Let me have a word with Rong," Shun went on to say, "and he will go ahead and prepare the way. Then we must converse before going up to the pavilions."

Shun took Rong aside and whispered, "Go quickly and tell Xiu he most hide. The storage room in the west wing is the best place. Tell him there will be no pirate captain for him to service this night. But do not tell him why or who the pirate is. Do you understand, Rong? Pay attention, Rong, this is very important."

Rong had been standing there, his eyes agape. The last time he'd seen this god of a man now called Ming Lei, the pirate, the man had been taking Rong's virginity. And afterward, Rong—like most of Niu's conquests—would have given anything to be taken again. When he focused on Shun, he simply muttered, "I do not understand."

"You need not understand," Shun hissed. "Just do as I say."

The zhaoguzhe did not have time or opportunity here on the dock in the dark, with the pirate captain just a few paces from them, to explain what had instantly come to him he must do—that he wanted to do. Shun, no less than Rong, had fallen under Niu's spell when he'd lost his virginity to the man. And he had chaffed, during months of service to the man, that Niu would not lie with him again thereafter—that he had eyes only for Xiu when they were still at the nanleshijia and could speak of no one but Xiu all the time they were tramping together

149

through the kingdom of Wu, trying to meet up with the king. Shun was flat out jealous and always would be. He no longer wanted to lie under Niu—or at least not as much as he once had. But he also didn't want Niu to have what he wanted—Xiu lying under him.

When Rong had started running up the stairs ascending the cliff to the men's pleasure house above, Shun went back to Niu's side.

"I am sorry, Niu—may we drop pretenses and call each other by the names we knew seasons ago?—but I have shocking news. We cannot go up the stairs before I've told you. You probably will not wish to go."

"What is it? I've come for the services of Xiu. You know that I want him."

"Xiu is no more, Niu."

"I do not understand. Explain yourself."

"Xiu died between the time your emissary visited us and now."

"How can this be? It has only been days."

"If I had known it was you, I could have saved you the trip. I know you only want virgins. Xiu was a bitten peach jinan, anyway. And that is why Xiu is no longer of this earth. You have heard of the fighting vessel of the Jin—the monster foreigners—kueilo—from the north that has been lurking in our waters."

"Yes, so? Do not tease with me. Your news has sorely wounded me."

"By the order of the Lord of Shi, Xiu's virginity was given to the kueilo captain. The clouds and rain ceremony was only two moons ago. But the hungmao—that is what we called him—was so massively built and so cruel that Xiu was torn asunder inside. He lingered from then until now, but he has succumbed from the servicing. You may remember Bolin. He too was ruined by the kueilo. He still breathes, but when you see how wounded he is, you will understand why Xiu passed on."

"This does not please me," Niu said angrily. "It does not please me one bit."

The zhaoguzhe looked at the man who had become a legendary pirate with concern. The nanleshijia was still in danger of being burned, it would seem. Shun did what he thought he had to do.

"We have young jinan in preparation who I am sure would please you—ones not yet bitten peaches. I would not have you come and be disappointed in having your need unmet."

"I have no time or patience for a formal clouds and rain ceremony with one of your uninitiated jinan. And I am in a foul mood now. I feel like conquering someone. Whatever the kueilo can do I can surpass."

Niu's eyes were full of anger and Shun knew that vengeance was on his mind. Thinking quickly, but not without regret, Shun sighed and said, "We have a young servant—just barely of age—who is comely and is a virgin. He appears a boy, but he is a man. He is shy and very innocent of the world. He is what I remember that you like. There need be no ceremony. You may do as you wish with him."

Shun regretted offering Tang like this. He was such a likable and trusting young man. Shun had been thinking of making him into a jinan, but he did not think the young man wanted that and he was really too old to start the long training process. But he was such an affable young man.

"My mood is to punish—to conquer . . . to lay ruin," Niu said grimly.

"We would not tell the young man what is to befall him, then," Shun said, with a deep sigh. "You could conquer him. Would that appease you? He belongs to the nanleshijia, so whatever you wish to do . . . whatever. He has no family. There is no one on earth who would know he ever existed."

* * * *

The jinan, Ping, was posed on a tatami mat on the decking outside the pavilion, singing a sad song and accompanying himself on the lute. Folds of silk robing swathed him from the waist down, cascading in folds around his kneeling body. His boyish, but well-muscled chest was bare and glistening with oil under the flickering lights of the torches.

Inside the dimly lit pavilion, a steaming tub of scented water had been prepared by the house servants, among them the shy Tang, who had been pointed out to the pirate captain when the servants had entered the room. The jinan, Wangan, was supervising the unrobing of Niu while the house servants prepared the bath. The scene had been orchestrated by Wangan, still smarting from how the kueilo captain had taken him by surprise in the tub. His mind had told him that if another one in the house of the Cut Sleeve was taken the same way, the embarrassing stories of his own ordeal would not be so baldly bandied about.

When Niu was naked, Wangan knelt before him and took Niu's magnificent yang chu in his mouth and gave him suck. After a few moments, with Niu in full erection, Wangan led Niu to the bath and helped him get into the tub and sit back. He sponged Niu's body off while the servants renewed the bath with hot water from jars. As the servants started to withdraw, Wangan took hold of Tang and crowded him against the side of the tub. Niu reach up under the hem of the young servant's tunic and took hold of his small cock. Tang gave an exclamation of surprise and Wangan took hold of the sides of the young servant's tunic and pulled it over his head and discarded it,

Tang began to whimper and to struggle, and Wangan pushed him into the tub with Niu and then turned and left. But he only went as far as through the beaded curtains to the corridor and then turned to watch from the shadows what would transpire. He'd heard the rumor that the cruel pirate had been given permission to take the unknowing servant to the grave. Such a story would completely eclipse the indignity that Wangan had suffered in that tub.

All the time Ping was singing his sad song and playing on his lute as if unaware of what was happening in the pavilion—although of course he knew what was happening.

Tang thrashed about on top of Niu in the tub, held there by Niu's strong encasing arms. Niu lowered his mouth Tang's nipples and bit him there, unconcerned and only laughing that Tang was flailing against him and had buried his hands in Niu's head hair. Niu's yang chu was between Tang's thighs, curving up into his buttocks and knocking for entrance, but the bulb was too big and Tang's virginal entrance was too small—and Tang was writhing and trying to get away, out of the tub.

Niu turned in the tub, getting Tang under him and pushed Tang's head under the water. He held it there for several seconds. When he pulled Tang's head up by his hair, the small, wild-eyed youth gasped for air, sputtered, and flung his body around.

After the third head dipping, though, all of the fight went out of Tang. Niu turned the young servant's body belly to the curve of the back of the tub, sternum against the rim, and arms dangling, useless and exhausted over the back of the tub. Tang looked to Ping with eyes that pleaded and showed his fear and lack of understanding of why this was happening to him. Ping cast his eyes down and continued singing his song and playing his lute. He knew what his position in the house was. He had not, however, been told that license had been given to take Tang beyond the pale.

Positioning his chest over Tang's back and kneeling behind him in the tub, with knees on either outer side of Tang's, Niu took his enormous, erect yang chu in his hand, positioned it at the young servant's virginal hole, and worked his way inside. Tang cried out, but Niu covered his mouth with his free hand and stifled off the young man's attempts to scream. He pinched the frightened servant's nose and completely covered the young man's mouth with the heel of his hand so that Tang nearly blacked out before Niu gave him momentary relief, toying with him, keeping the young man barely conscious.

Wanting more play from his prey, Niu released Tang's mouth and nose, and the young servant gasped, taking in great gulps of air. Niu reached around and slapped Tang on the face, trying to make him more animated, more resistant, regardless of how futile that was. Tang began a half-hearted attempt to struggle again, as Niu's cock slowly worked its way inside him, but his writhing only served to saddle Niu more quickly. Niu's hands when to Tang's throat and applied pressure, giving the young servant something else to worry about—where his next breath was coming from—more than the gigantic staff that had taken possession of his channel.

Niu began to pump, slowly at first and then faster and faster, working out all of the anger he felt at the loss of Xiu. Tang lay under him, inert, no longer struggling, and when Niu let loose of his throat and moved a hand to cup the young man's chin and arch his head backward, Tang took Niu's thumb inside his mouth with no more than a whimper and gave it suck.

By the time Niu had given the erstwhile virgin his seed, Tang was moaning and sighing and his hips were moving in rhythm with Niu's thrusting pelvis.

Rising up from the tub, Niu declared, "That was satisfying, but nothing will substitute for the loss of the dead Xiu."

Ping looked up sharply. Tang wasn't dead, and it seemed that the pirate was finished toying with him. But, more important, Xiu wasn't dead. Niu apparently thought Xiu was dead, but Ping knew he wasn't. And Ping had been in the nanleshijia when Niu had been here as baoan and had lost his position because he was randy for Xiu, who had not been through the cloud and rain ceremony yet. After Niu had escaped north from the nanleshijia with the current zhaoguzhe, Shun, as his servant, Ping knew that Xiu had pined for Niu.

Ping had experienced his own lost love. The son of the cotton industrialist, who had claimed to love him but who had deserted him when he found out Ping was a jinan—and had been his father's jinan.

When he was sold back to the Cut Sleeve Nanleshijia, Ping had repeatedly been told that he had violated one of the key rules of the world of the jinan—he had made the mistake of loving a man. But Ping, even though he had been deserted by his love, rebelled against this "rule." The life of a jinan was rough and tragic and they all either died young or were turned into old, bitter men with nothing but the most servile duties ahead of them. Ping would take any chance at love rather than never having loved at all.

He knew that Xiu loved Niu. Xiu had pined for Niu for months after the baoan has left. The lives of so many of the jinan turned to tragedy, as Ping well knew, and he wished that one—just one—of his fellow cut sleeves could receive happiness.

The zhaoguzhe returned to the pavilion. "I hope that our precious servant, Tang, has satisfied your needs, sire," Shun said, his eyes downcast. He didn't want to look at the unwitting servant who he had given to Niu, although in his heart he was relieved that the young man still was breathing. Tang was silent, only half conscious and exhausted, still draped over the edge of the tub where Niu had left him. But he was alive. Shun hoped the young man would never know what could have been his fate.

Shun took another look at Tang—and was rewarded with a pin prick of slight disgust—when he saw Tang lift his eyes and look dreamily at Niu. A slight smile formed on the spent youth's mouth. Yet another fool to have lost his virginity to Niu, Shun thought, and roughly so—but who would gladly open his legs to Niu again if given the chance.

"He does not suffice for Xiu, no," Niu said gruffly. "But I have changed since you last knew me. If a virgin has pleased me, I will lay with him again. If you give Tang to me to take back to my ship and dally with, I will not further show my displeasure for the loss of Xiu. But I am still wild with grief that he is beyond the pale."

Fearing the pirate captain's wrath, Shun reluctantly agreed to give him Tang. He tried his best not to look at Tang, but he could not help doing so, and, as he knew would be the case, Tang was now looking well pleased.

The zhaoguzhe left the pavilion to summon Wangan to prepare Tang for travel.

This left Niu and the semicomatose Tang alone with Ping.

Understanding that Niu loved Xiu as Xiu loved Niu—and that Niu would not reject Xiu just because Xiu was no longer a virgin—and driven by his bitterness over how a jinan was supposed to see love of a jinan for a man, Ping stopped singing and said softly, not even meaning Niu to hear him, "Xiu is not dead."

But Niu heard him. "What is that you have said, singer?"

"Xiu is not dead. He is here in this nanleshijia—and very much alive. I can take you to him," Ping said in a stronger voice.

When they reached the storage room in the west wing, Niu still naked, not having robed in his excitement at being taken to Xiu, beat down the door that locked Xiu away. Ping stepped back, as the two lovers, in instant recognition, rushed into each other's arms like two bulls fighting over a cow. They kissed wildly as Niu tore at Xiu's robes. Still standing, Niu pushed Xiu's body against the wall, Xiu climbed Niu's hips with his legs, and Niu quickly was fucking Xiu in long, insistent, deep thrusts.

Ping returned to the pavilion where Tang had been ravished. Wangan was there, drying and clucking soothing noises at the trembling body of Tang, no longer in the tub.

"The pirate is not here," Wangan said sharply to Ping as he reentered the pavilion.

"He is gone, back to his ship," Ping said, knowing for a certainty that this would be true as soon as the two lovers had reached their initial explosion. And Ping knew that Xiu would be going with Niu.

"Back to his ship?" Tang raised his head and plaintively whispered. "But he said he was going to take me with him."

And, looking at the crushed expression on Tang's face, Ping too now knew that the mystique of Niu continued. Every virgin he conquered wanted more of him.

Shun entered the pavilion at that moment, and upon hearing the news that Niu was gone, his face showed the same utter disappointment as Tang's did.

The zhaoguzhe, Ping thought, even he remains under the spell of Niu.

* * * *

156

Not more than an hour later, the alarm bell was ringing at the entrance of the nanleshijia. Shun, Rong, and the jinan and servants were slow to react, as they were still reeling from searching for Niu and not finding him—and then discovering that Xiu was gone as well. It would not have mattered if they were on full alert, though. The nanleshijia was quickly overrun with the crew of the Jin fighting ship.

The raiders of the Jin ship had arrived earlier than expected and had arrived randy, having heard the tales of pleasure their hungmao captain and gold-haired first mate had told of their visit to the Cut Sleeve Nanleshijia.

The gold-haired monster grabbed Shun by the wrist and threatened his life if he did not reveal where Bolin was being kept. Out of fear for his master, Rong, told the gold-hair where he could find the jinan who was still recovering from the kueilo's last visit.

The gold-hair handed Shun over to two burly sailors, with another set taking Rong, and both were floored and double fucked where they had stood. Both Wangan and Tang were back in the tub of water, one draped over one end and the other over the other, each with a sailor pumping their asses.

The hungmao was standing before Ping who had returned to his tatami mat and his song and lute while the others of the house had been frantically and unsuccessfully searching for Niu and Xiu.

The Jin boat captain smiled cruelly at Ping, shrugged out of his clothing, and grabbed his yang chu in his hand.

Ping had played his music for the hungmao and Xiu during Xiu's clouds and rain initiating ceremony and had seen the foreigner's body and yang chu in all of their magnificence. He had heard Xiu moan for the hungmao as he had moaned for no one else when Ping was playing for Xiu while he entertained a client. And Ping knew how deeply Xiu had fantasized about this foreign devil's prowess when he had returned to his ship.

Resigned to his lot in life and how few useful years he had left in his profession—and already torched by love—Ping smiled back at the hungmao, opened his robes, took up a pillow, and laid back on the tatami mat, with the pillow under the small of his back. He lifted and spread his legs.

The hungmao came to him quickly, reached under Ping's legs and spread his buttocks cheeks, placed the bulb of his staff at Ping's opening, and began to push.

Ping panted and moaned, wondering how Xiu was able to endure this, knowing that he couldn't. But then he could, and the hungmao was plowing him deep. Ping groaned and cried out in pain melding into pleasure, the most possession he'd ever felt, and began to move his hips in consort with the hungmao's thrusting pelvis and to work the hungmao's yang chu with the undulating muscles of his channel walls. The hungmao gasped and laughed and began pumping in earnest.

Ping could hear the plaintive wailing of Bolin in his faraway room, having been found in his sick bed, still there from the last brutal assault on his body by the gold-haired kueilo. But Ping didn't care. He was receiving the clouds and rain of a lifetime. If he were to die now, he would not care.

But Ping was not to die now. The debauchery coming to a close, the sailors were choosing their captives. The gold-hair was striding toward the nanleshijia's entrance with an unconscious Bolin slung over his shoulder.

The hungmao gave the command to fire the pavilions, and sailors had already started doing that. The hungmao, however, fucked on. Ping had come twice for him and had maneuvered the kueilo into the position of the beaten dog, which gave both more pleasure and the hungmao even more depth inside Ping.

At the last possible moment, after lathering Ping's insides with his cum, the hungmao laughed and rose from Ping. For an instant, Ping thought he'd be left there to burn, but then the hungmao reached down, picked Ping up—with Ping reaching out and grabbing his lute as he was being raised—and slung Ping over his shoulder.

The crew of the Jin fighting ship was gone from the burning nanleshijia compound as quickly as they had appeared.

Shun and Rong were both among those left behind. They struggled up and stumbled out of the burning pavilion.

Pulling themselves together, they began organizing an effort to save whatever of the other pavilions could be saved.

The next morning Shun was standing out on the deck on the cliff overlooking the bend in the Yangtze. He had his back to the smoldering remains of his compound. His mind was assessing what he had left in terms of jinan, servants, and pavilion space. The raiders had not found the house's treasure store. It obviously had been other treasure they were randy for.

Rong had been sent to the prefecture capital at Yangzhou to inform the Lord of Shi of the debauching by the foreign devils. But for the Cut Sleeve Nanleshijia, at least, any military response to the foreign raid would be too little, too late.

The Jin fighting ship was out there, taunting the people of the Middle Kingdom. Shun could see the masts of the giant ship near the mouth of the Yangtze. Not wanting to look to where who knows what was happening to his lost jinan, Shun looked up river. He saw that the pirate ship of Ming Lei, who he knew as Niu, was sailing back down the river toward the mouth of the Yangtze. By now Shun had guessed that Niu had found Xiu and had taken him away to his ship. Shun also surmised that Xiu had gone willingly. He could not fault Xiu. If Niu beckoned to Shun, even now, Shun would go with him too.

With a jolt, Shun realized that the pirate ship was headed for the Jin fighting ship. His first thought was to descend to the dock and to try to signal Niu's ship somehow that he was sailing into the arms of a foreign fighting ship of immense size and power. Shun had no idea who would win in a battle between these two.

He started to move toward the top of the stairs down the side of the cliff, but then he stopped. He realized that he really didn't care. All he really cared about was the welfare of his jinan—and most of them were beyond his help now. He sighed, thinking of the old saying that jinan were lucky if they died young, because their glory came early, flared for a few short years, and then it was all emptiness after that. So, the lucky jinan died young. Most of them died tragically.

Shun turned his face away from the river and walked slowly back into the ashes of the nanleshijia. Whatever drama was about to be played out at the mouth of the Yangtze was beyond his control—or his care.

The Beautiful Way Identified Characters

Bolin: male prostitute (Gentle Rain) (pronounced as written, with a long "o")

Deming: male prostitute initiate (Virtue Bright) (pronounced "duh meeng")

Deng Qiao: Nantung cotton mill owner (Qiao = Proud) (pronounced "dung chow")

Duke of Shi: ruler of the prefecture of Nanfeng ("shi" pronounced "sher")

Fu Yang: a rice merchant (Rich Sun) (pronounced "foo yahng")

Hsiang: master of the Golden Peach theater troupe (pronounced "shee ahng")

Jiayi: third son of the King of Wu (pronounced "gee ah yee")

King of Wu: Jili, monarch of the state of Wu (pronounced "woo")

Meilin: wife of Deng Qiao (Plum Grove) (pronounced "may lynn")

Ming Lei: notorious sea pirate (Thunder Dynasty) (pronounced "meeng lie")

Niu: male brothel protector (the Ox) (pronounced "new")

Longwei: son of the cotton mill owner Deng Qiao (pronounced "long why")

Lord of Anyi: Zhu Xin Yi, ruler of a prefecture on the Wu-Chu border (name pronounced "chu she yee"; "chu" pronounced "choo")

Pai: male prostitute (pronounced "pie")

Ping: male prostitute (Tranquillity) (pronounced "peeng")

Rong: a young soldier in the army of the King of Wu (Honor) (pronounced "roong")

Shun: a brothel servant, later manager (Obedient) (pronounced as spelled)

Tang: a young servant of the Cut Sleeve male brothel (pronounced "dawng")

the zhaoguzhe: manager of the male brothel (pronounced "zow goo she")

Wangan: male prostitute (pronounced "wang ahn")

Wangtao: a procurer (pronounced "wang dow")

Xiaodan: male prostitute (Little Dawn) (pronounced "shou [as in "shout"] "dan")

Xiu: male prostitute (Fine Beauty) (pronounced "shoe")

Yongrui: former lover of the Nantung cotton mill owner Deng Qiao (pronounced "yawng rhu")

Zhu Xin Yi: Lord of Anyi

The Beautiful Way Glossary of Chinese and Key Terms

Aeiii: Oh! (pronounced "aye ee")

Baoan: protector (pronounced ("bow" [as in a dog's bark] "ahn")

bitten peach: a man initiated in man-on-man sex

chenchieh: chastity (pronounced "jin jee")

chench'an: war ship (pronounced "jin jew ahn")

chi'en: money (pronounced "chee in")

ching pu: please don't (pronounced "ching boo")

chiu: rice wine (pronounced "joe")

ch'an: sailing vessel (pronounced "chu wan")

ch'uanchu: ship's captain (pronounced "chew ahn jew")

Chungkuojen: Chinese men (pronounced "jewng gwoo rin")

clouds and rain: the completed sex act; clouds = fucking, rain = ejaculation/orgasm

cut sleeve: a male prostitute

Floating World: the world of prostitution

fu chin: father (pronounced "foo gin")

hanfu: ceremonial robes (pronounced "hawn foo")

hen da: too big (pronounced "hun dah")

hen hao: very good (pronounced "hun how")

hsieh, hsieh: thanks (pronounced "shyeh shyeh")

hsienchien: cash money (pronounced "shin chee in")

hsien sheng: mister (pronounced "shin shung")

hungmao: red-haired devil (pronounced "hung maow")

jen: men (pronounced "rin")

jinan: male prostitute (pronounced "chee ahn")

kueilo: foreign ghosts (non-Chinese) (pronounced "kway low")

land of Jin: foreign land to the north of China. In the vicinity of present-day Korea or the Kamchatka peninsula.

laoshi: master teacher (pronounced "lao sher")

mu chin: mother (pronounced "moo gin")

nanleshijia: male brothel (pronounced "nan lee sher geeah")

peach: a ripe, young, virginal man

pu yao: it's not (pronounced "pooh ya ow")

shangchu'an: merchant ship (pronounced "shang jew ahn")

shih: yes (pronounced "sher")

Shunga: Japanese underworld; erotic art (pronounced "shun gaw")

ta ao: cotton long coat (pronounced "da ow")

The Beautiful Way: male prostitution

tuan ku: loin cloth (pronounced "two ahn goo")

yang chu: cock (pronounced "yang jew")

zhaodaojen: procurer (pronounced "tsa ow do wren")

zhaoguzhe: caretaker (pronounced "tsa ow goo gee")

About the Author

Dirk Hessian

An artist and writer, Dirk has always been interested in history and legends, particularly those of the United States, the Mediterranean, and Asia. His works are historical, and sometimes border on fantasy. They are full of ordinary men struggling to survive and find love in difficult situations. And sometimes Dirk writes about men who are in touch with forces beyond those of mortal men, fighting for survival in more unusual ways.

Dirk's books often, but not always, contain male sex that is both forceful and rough, and at times dangerous, but is always within the context of stories of survival in more primitive and brutal times. He also writes about the power of love in turbulent times.

He can be found at the adults only gay male site www.BarbarianSpy.com, which he shares with Sabb and habu (sr71plt).

Our authors always like to receive feedback, and appreciate it when readers post reviews to BarbarianSpy, Goodreads, Amazon, and other review sites.

BarbarianSpy
FOR LITERARY HEAT

Not all books listed below may currently be on release.
* indicates the book is available in paperback and e-book.

BOOKS BY DIRK HESSIAN
Xtreme Erotica
The King's Men
Shores of Tripoli
Prophecy of Noto
Pretender's Fate
General Erotica/Romance
Fire Down the Valley*
Constantinople*
The Beautiful Way*
Blue and Gray
Colonel's Treasure
Beginning of Time
Labyrinth

BOOKS BY HABU
Gay Erotica
Memoir Faction
Flying High, Diving Deep*
Xtreme Erotica
Apyko: The Greek Pimp
Visits of the Schlange
Second Coming: Emile La Cour Unleashed
Vortex: Sacrificed by Curiosity*
Dark Angel Sounding (in e-book & included in
Sounding:Ultimate Control Paperback)*
Sounding: Ultimate Control (Print Only)*
Sounding Five (in e-book & included in
Sounding:Ultimate Control paperback)*
General Erotica
Romance
Snowy, Snowy Nights (Christmas Romance)

Four Coins
Lower Than the Heart
Brambleton
Gotta Keep Trying
Finding Amnad
Platres Conclave
Other Novels/Novellas
Cruising Gigolo
Prepared in Cape Verdi
Gilded Cage
House on Park
Anything for Ambition
Dance of the Ravishers
Hard Knocks U*
My Neighbor's Spa*
Man's Man: Tales of a High Priced Gay Hooker*
Trip Money
Clint Folsom Mysteries Compendium Volume 1*
Death to Blonds - Stolen Judgment (Clint Folsom
Mystery)*
Clint Folsom Mysteries Compendium Volume 2*
The Indian Doctor
Sailorboy
Home to Fire Island
Choke Hold
Gay Erotica Anthologies
Spy Tails 001*
Spy Tails 002*
Doubled*
Doubled Again*
Tails in the Tropics*
Tails in the Med*
Tails in the West*
Rough Riders*
Grab Bag 1*
Grab Bag 2*
Grab Bag 3*
Grab Bag 4*

Grab Bag 5*
Beyond the Beaded Curtain*
Habu's Christmas Balls
The Sporting Life*
Fetish Galore!*
Literary Gay Erotica
Cairo Surrender*
The Handyman*
Homeward Bound
Journey to Mirage*
Menage Erotica
Cruising Gigolo
13 Ways for Halloween
Luther*
The Indian Prince
Literary GLBT Fiction
Summer of Denial
BOOKS BY SHABBU
Finding Jason
Dirty Pool
Operation Black Jade
Cigars!*
Angel in the Barn
Gayly Complicated*
Despoiling David
The Tree of Idleness*
I Met a Man
The Interview
Rough Road to Happiness
BOOKS BY SABB
Hiring in Hollywood
The Legend of Holleystone Grange
Surprise Encounters
She is He
Wrong Man
Loyal to his King
Barbarian Tales - Book One - Traveler's Tales*
Barbarian Tales - Book Two - Journeys Begin*

Barbarian Tales - Book Three - The Inheritance*
Barbarian Tales - Book Four - Road to Persepolis*